The Essence

Book Four of the Unity Chronicles

By

Graham Mann

The Essence

Book Four of the Unity Chronicles

Prologue

Won'Kaat Station

"You're new," said the gruff barkeep. He was a sturdy, bearded man - with bloodshot eyes that peered out from beneath the mess of dishevelled brown hair, which partially obscured his uneven features. The pungent stench of Reed smoke clung to his breath, "So, what brings you here?"

"New Unity business," Treelo replied, "I am an ambassador, here to spread the word of peace to the darker parts of the galaxy. This establishment looked like the ideal place to start."

"I'd keep your voice down if I were you. You could attract yourself a whole lot of trouble talking like that."

"Well, there's no-one else in here, and besides, a little trouble isn't so bad. It gives me an excuse to stay amongst the action... if you get my meaning."

"You are certainly an unusual type to be visiting *Won'Kaat Station*. This establishment also offers undertaking services... if you want to plan ahead, or speeder retrofitting if you want to run, which in my opinion would be the better option for you." The barkeep did a wheezy laugh, which swiftly became a hacking cough.

"I don't think that'll be necessary. I wonder, do you know anything of Kan Vok Tah? I have heard whispers that he is here-abouts."

"Kan Vok Tah eh? You here for sexual deviance, drugs or revenge? It's always one of the three."

"Well...actually he's my father." The barkeep raised a curious eyebrow, "Just kidding, it's none of those reasons. Just a courtesy visit. It's part of my civic duty as an ambassador," Treelo smiled, as he tapped his empty glass on the bar top to request a refill. The barkeep obliged, and left the uncorked bottle on the counter.

"Does that civic duty include running up a gigantic Raktee bill?" he asked.

"Perks of the job, I get expenses paid. I'm an ambassador… not a saint," he laughed.

"To answer your question," replied the barkeep, "Even if I did know where he was, I'm not stupid enough to tell you, or anyone else who comes in here asking. You don't meddle in Kan Vok Tah's affairs. Asking questions like that will most definitely lead you to having a use for our aforementioned undertaking services."

"That's a shame, we're old friends," lied Treelo.

"*Huh hmm.*" A new voice joined the conversation.

"Pardon my rude interruption, I couldn't help but overhear that you are an ambassador for the New Unity. I for one think that what you are doing for the galaxy in the name of peace is nothing short of outstanding," said the stranger, who spoke in sycophantic tones.

"I appreciate your approval, friend. I am Treelo, and you are?"

"My name is Daa'Shond," said the sly-looking stranger. "And this barkeep here is lying to you. This is in fact, Kan Vok Tah's place. He is in the back room, counting his ill- gotten gains no doubt." The barkeep's face dropped.

"Thank you, friend" said Treelo.

"Oh, the pleasure is all mine. I'll keep an eye on our less-than-honest friend here, whilst you go about your business. Be warned though, he has two of his undesirables in there with him."

"Why are you helping me?", Treelo asked.

"The right outcome here today could prove very beneficial for me." Daa'Shond smiled viciously, "I'm a chancer, not a saint. Mwah!" he said, raising a knowing eyebrow.

* * * * * * * * * *

After spending a few moments suppressing his newly gained morals and gathering some courage, Treelo left his seat at the bar and headed for the back rooms. He knew that what he meant to do here today went against everything the New Unity stood for. But in truth, he felt that he had no choice. He'd made a promise years ago, and now that the opportunity to keep it had arisen, he wasn't about to pass it up.
Treelo eased a heavy set of doors open - to be met by a holographic wonderland of visual delights, strippers, live sex bots, (all species were catered for here), but none of it was real. It was no more than a collection of vulgarities to enhance the masturbating habits

of any would-be punters. Treelo moved through the room – undeterred by the 'attractions' his mind was focused on one thing. At the next set of doors, what Treelo was confronted with felt altogether different, darker and heavier…

****

The bloated, sweaty pig that was Kan Vok Tah, sat smugly at the counting table within his private room at the back of the club. He had relocated his *business* after the crackdown on Sin. The ex-industrial asteroid was now just another cold, uninhabited chunk of rock, floating silently through space. That forsaken place could tell a million tales if it had a voice. But, Kan Vok's *business* was the type that didn't stay shut down for long. He named his newest establishment after that rock: a homage to his former home. His unique brand of debauchery, and his blatant disregard for the law, were in great demand among the darker, more desperate beings of the galaxy. He had replicated his seedy gambling den here on *Won'kaat Station* to great effect.

Treelo stood outside the doors, allowing himself a moment to gain some much-needed composure, and to get the adrenaline surge that flooded through his body and mind under control. He drew his blaster, and with a very deep breath, kicked the heavy doors open.
    "KAN VOK TAH!" he shouted as he charged into the dingey room. His weapon was powered up, ready to cause some serious damage.
    "Remember me?" It was more of a command than a question.
    "Can't say I do," Kan Vok Tah replied, without so much as an upward glance. Tam

flicked a credit to one of Kan Vok's thugs.

"Here, bury him somewhere nice." Now Kan Vok's attention had been caught. Those were the exact words the man himself had used; and the very same credit he had flicked to Tam all those years ago, just seconds before he had murdered Neela in cold blood. He had attempted to kill Treelo too.

"Actually, it is coming back to me, my would-be friend," he laughed, "You are supposed to be dead, like that treacherous, runaway whore Neela. It's nice of you to come back so that I can finish the job off properly. Will you pair of humourless grunts just kill hi..." The fizz and static of blaster fire crackled through the air, before he could finish his overly-confident speech]. Kan Vok Tah's head lurched back with such force, that the resulting ricochet sent his whole upper body and fat head thudding face-first into the counting table. A slew of blood and gore oozed from the gaping wound where his cranium used to be. The guards dropped their weapons in surrender.

"Good choice," said Treelo, "I'm going to leave now. I was never here, okay?" The guards shrugged; there was no loyalty amongst their kind, and nothing to be gained from defending a dead boss.

"We won't mourn him," said the larger of the two guards in a thick, gravel-filled voice, "Neela was a friend to us all. He got what he had coming to him." Treelo nodded his head cautiously as he backed out of the room, closing the heavy doors behind him. He turned and ran through the mini red-light district, bursting through the next set of doors to re-enter the bar. He was met with a startling sight: the barkeep's corpse sat slumped on a bar stool. The word *Liar* had been carved deep into his forehead. Blood ran from the fresh wounds, and pooled in the sockets of his still open eyes. Treelo presumed this was the handy work of the mysterious Daa'Shond, who was nowhere to be seen. Treelo cautiously approached the victim.

"Sorry you got caught up in this mess," he addressed the barkeep's corpse apologetically. He grabbed the bottle of Raktee from the bar top, taking a deep swig.

"On the upside, it's better than the slow asphyxiation caused by Reed addiction." Treelo gently closed the dead man's eyes. He needed to leave now. He pulled up his hood, obscuring his face, and stealthily exited the scene. He vanished, bottle in hand, into the bustle of the crowds that populated the station.

Chapter One

Reconciliation

Two months earlier

Almost three years after the defeat of the
Raize, the New Unity was enjoying a period of
peace and prosperity. Some might call it
utopian even. *Veela VI* had a strong population
of Veel'aans, (some born of the Genesis
Sphere's bio-pod generation), and many
Veel'aans thought to be long dead had returned
from the darkest nooks and distant corners of
the galaxy. The R'aal dwelled peacefully in
The Silence of Veela. After the Battle Of
Mora, they had requested to be cut off from
the rest of the planet, and had also asked not
to be drawn into any future conflicts. The
only people they had seen since were Gliis and
Kee'Pah - on their many explorations deep into
the caves. On the opposite side of the
mountains, an expansive development of new
homesteads littered the surface of the planet,
augmented with raw Vee'Laan core matter, and
powered by planetary energy. These new
structures blended seamlessly with the
restored buildings of the old town and village
square. Ancient artworks and treasures had
been excavated, and now hung or stood proudly

on display in the public galleries of the new town. All of this was set against the spectacle of the Stadia Terranus: an ancient amphitheater gifted to the people by the planet. *Veela VI* was set to become a popular tourist destination for Unitians galaxy-wide.

This growth and renewal wasn't just happening on Veela VI. The New Unity as a whole was growing and flourishing. Nataalu's outlook as leader could be best described as impatiently hopeful and optimistic. Although she had picked up her fair share of doubters along the way, many calling her overly-confident and callous in her wishes to celebrate and embrace the peace time.

You can never please everyone all of the time, just follow your heart. Those were the wise words of her once clueless brother Taire, during the most recent of their sporadic communications. He had changed so much over the years. He was now a full-grown man, a leader, and an accomplished warrior. It seemed, to her, a waste of his talents that he was on a constant perimeter sweep in the outer edges of the system. He could be training and mentoring the next generations of young Unitians. Nataalu wasn't a fan of the distance that she and her siblings had been asked to place between them, although she understood the reasoning behind the request. She had never gotten used to having to bend to the wants and needs of a paranoid council… and it was wearing. These thoughts played heavily on her mind, and to add to that pressure, Tecta had summoned her to the training grounds for a long, over-due workout. Even though it had been three years since Tecta returned from his self-imposed exile, it pained her that their

relationship had remained fractured and
distant. She, however, wasn't blameless for
that.

* * * * * * * * * *

Lu entered the clearing deep within the
Monl'aal mountain range of *Veela VI*, where
Tecta would be lying in wait. The ever-
predictable ambush would no doubt be his
opening gambit.

"Greetings Nataalu, it pleases me to see
you." She was surprised to see that Tecta just
stood there in the centre of the clearing.
"What's this, no ambush?" she replied.
Tecta activated the automated cannons embedded
in the training grounds as she spoke. Lu leapt
left and right, dodging the blasts.
"How have you been?" Tecta asked dryly.
"Me? I'm wonderful, honestly. Apparently,
I'm running the risk of becoming a strong-
minded but soft-bellied diplomat. Those are
the words I heard they are using?" Lu's
response came in a broken sentence between
deflecting blasts. Her words contained sass
and hurt in equal measure, as she spat them
out amid multiple leaps and evasive
manoeuvres. "*Empathiser*, they use that word as
an insult." She aggressively deflected volley
after volley of training bolts, "If we don't
have empathy, we have nothing." She made a
controlled descent to the dusty ground,
already taking up her attack stance.
"I'm sure they meant no offence, besides I
can see that you are putting your annoyance to
good use… so technically." Tecta paused to
block Lu's incoming strike, "They've motivated
you." She lunged at him - her strikes were
coming as thick and fast as her words now.

"We need to offer a real alternative: there are addicts who need support, the poor and the vulnerable are still being abused. We cannot pick and choose; we have sworn to be an inclusive society, abolishing oppression and bringing the oppressors to justice." Tecta repeatedly dodged, ducked, parried and countered.

"They may not want an alternative. They may be happy with their life choices." Tecta was clearly playing devil's advocate.

"Well, the least we can do is offer them realistic choices. I can only lead in a way that I see fit!"

"I understand and admire your insight. But, be aware that some situations you cannot talk your way out of, and sometimes you will still need to fight. This is a lesson you learned long ago. I'm merely jogging your memory to keep you sharp. Maybe they've forgotten your past battles and triumphs in the wake of your growing wisdom."

"So patronising," sneered Lu, "I've been fighting ever since we left you on *Veela VI*." She activated anti-grav mode on her combat suit, and leapt high into the air. She pushed off one rock face into a tuck, ricocheted off the adjacent outcrop, and engaging thrusters, she darted downward straight towards Tecta – both fists outstretched firing training bolts. Tecta deflected the seemingly endless barrage then caught Lu by the fists… they were lost in his gargantuan palms. He held her gaze intently, while her boosters continued blasting.

"I did not appoint myself leader!" Lu screamed, attempting to push Tecta back, "I seem to recall that was your doing. Just like when you decided to leave!!" Lu was breathing hard through gritted teeth, shaking with anger and exertion. She disengaged thrusters and anti-grav mode, slowly lowering her feet to the ground.

"And I stand by those decisions, as I stand by you now. So stop complaining and defend yourself!" It was Tecta's turn to be the aggressor once again, levelling his wrist blasters at Lu. She turned and flipped in retreat. Tecta released a rapid volley of shots. Nataalu repelled them in turn, as if brushing aside a meagre annoyance.

"It's been three years since the Raize, and you are still so paranoid! What really happened to you on *Antipathy*?" she bellowed, as she strode defiantly towards him.

"Stop projecting, this isn't about me," snapped Tecta.

"Are you sure? You seem to make almost everything about you these days. Why can we not relish in the peaceful time we currently live in? Or celebrate our achievements and help those in need? Maybe I could even see my brothers. Taire is out there being a security guard to the whole galaxy, whilst Gliis rarely breaks the surface of Unity. He and Kee have become practically subterranean and obsessive in their quest for ancient knowledge, and on whose orders?! Huh? Why can't we just enjoy life once in a while?" Lu's response stung Tecta; he expected her to vent, and he knew that she needed to get many things off her chest. He also knew that she made a valid argument. He deactivated his training program and slumped down on the nearest rock.

"From what I have seen in the other star systems, there is much to fear - and many a threat that may see us as a bountiful target. Also, the Feruccian people still live, and as relieved as I am that I did not commit genocide, I have clearly made us the primary target for their wrath. But most troubling of all is Nel's warning of the Dark Mother. I cannot shake the feeling that the answer to our prolonged protection against her - is out there somewhere in the other systems." Tecta looked skyward as he spoke; he was, after all, just living up to his name, (or Gliis' childhood version of it.) He had, and always would be, a Protector Droid.

"It seems that you and I both needed this," Lu smiled, almost sadly, "Why is this *feeling* that you have so different to any of your previous hunches?" said Lu. Her anger had subsided at the sight of vulnerability from Tecta. He was so many things to her: mentor, critic, trainer, friend, and by no means least - he was a father figure. Without his love, guidance and selflessness, she and her brothers would have perished long ago, and the New Unity would have been nothing more than an unrealised pipe dream. Tecta saw the depth and expression in Lu's eyes.

"And there she is, my daughter Nataalu," Tecta smiled warmly.

"We will be ready father. If and when any of these threats may come near New Unity's way, we will face them together. Maybe you should use this peaceful time to explore your hunch? Go to the other system, and see what you can learn there. I'm surprised you haven't already reached this conclusion."

"I have my child, though I could not face telling you, or your brothers, that I need to leave once more."

"We have grown up. We will stay on our guard, but we will also embrace our hard-earned peace, and use it to good effect. You need to take this opportunity, whilst the system is settled, to go in search of the answers that you believe can aid us. We will be here waiting when you return."

"And what will you do about your critics, and their inevitable outrage that you have suggested such a thing?"

"The same as I always do, whatever is best for them, despite the doubters' misgivings about me." She sighed in acceptance of that fact.

"You are a beacon of shining light in this galaxy Nataalu, never lose sight of that. It may be your greatest gift. So realise your dream, and let us put this peace-time to good use. But, when the time comes to fight, which it inevitably will, be fearless my child - and burn bright. I am so proud of you."

"You forgot to mention my penchant for displaying sulky, brattish behaviour when left unchecked for too long," Lu laughed playfully.

"Come, I must go visit with Vrin. She always has an insight on my 'hunches' as you call them."

"You are not wrong about that… and Tecta?"

"Yes Nataalu?"

"Thank you."

"No, my child, I must thank you. It seems your wisdom has surpassed my own."

"One more thing… make sure that you are back in time for the party."

"Party?"

"Pilot's celebration of course," she smiled cheekily.

"I'll have to be," said Tecta, "I'm taking him with me."

* * * * * * * * * *

Pilot had been officially hailed as the Sixth Child of the New Unity: a bonafide element of the prophecy. In Nataalu's mind, there had never been any doubt that this would come to be. Pilot, however, had taken some convincing. Finally, he had accepted the title, and then proceeded to share said title with every member of the Pilot race.

"Pilots as one are Six Child."

Pilot's ascension was indeed cause for celebration. Lu was right; there was a long, over-due, party to be had, and what better venue than the rejuvenated planet of *Veela VI*?

"Send invitations to the Children of the New Unity… we are going to celebrate Pilot's ascension where this whole journey began - right here on *Veela VI*, in the Stadia Terranus. The planet has gifted this beautiful structure to us, and we shall use it." For the first time in a very long time, Nataalu dared to smile, and not hide it.

"What's the point in winning our freedom, if we are too afraid to live a little, and celebrate our triumphs?"

Chapter Two

The Twisted, The Bad And The Downright Hideous

After the destruction of *Antipathy*, Daa'Shond led a nomadic existence, but he hadn't rested on his laurels. He'd been single- minded in his mission, and now after three long years, his plans were on the verge of coming to fruition. He had scoured the galaxy recruiting anyone that had been wronged by the New Unity. Daa'Shond had researched and recruited a selection of the most unsavoury characters in the galaxy. He'd found Vrex, (the right-hand man of Injis), stranded on a distant moon… feasting on his own flesh to survive. He had heard the tale of Son Reynar and his mauling at the hands of Taire, and most tantalisingly delicious of all, he had tracked down the last remaining Feruccians - who had survived Tecta's deceptive assault on their homeworld. This night was to mark the long-awaited culmination of his plans.

* * * * * * * * * *

"I have secured a base of operations: it is finally time for our meeting of minds. I am eager to see what each of you brings to the table. The more cruel and unusual the better. This New Unity has wronged each of us in myriad ways, hence the invitation I extend to each of you. I mean to help you take back what is rightfully yours." Daa'Shond's pinched, nasal voice was full of confidence, and carried an air of intentional, overblown arrogance.

"I've known you marginally longer than the others in this conversation," Vrex grunted, "And I'm sure that they are as intrigued as I to understand what's in this for you? You are, after all, not even of this star system." Vrex's image on the comms screen was more hideous, more scarred, pock-marked and raw than ever.

"As I have said, the New Unity has wronged us all. I simply wish to take pleasure in being part of this delicious act of revenge. I have provided you with the coordinates, though I'm sure that this place is known to you all."

"*Won'kaat Station,*" - you could almost feel Son Reynar's sneer as his thick voice came through the comms - "I don't hate this idea, hiding in plain sight. Who else will be joining us for this 'meeting of minds?'

"No-one with any sense. From what I've heard, it's a miracle that piece of crap hasn't imploded yet," said Vrex.

"Does Kan Vok Tah not have the monopoly on that station?" added Son Reynar.

"Don't give Tah a second thought. He has been... how shall I put it? *Permanently evicted…* mwah!" Daa'Shond's smugness seemed to know no bounds, "Although I admit the station is a little run-down, it has a certain antiquated charm. Besides, its clientele are exactly the type of putrid slime we need."

"Speaking of slime, have you reached out to the Slaavene?" asked Son Reynar, the air of distaste in his tone blatantly apparent.

"I have been advised that they are not to be trusted in the current climate. I believe the term that was used was thus - *They should have two faces instead of two hearts* - Did I get that right, brother Azvoc? Mwah!" Daa'Shond's stilted laugh set Son Reynar's teeth on edge.

"Yes Daa'Shond, word-perfect; they are treacherous, slithering filth." The voice that spoke was an unfamiliar one.

"In light of the events on my home *Antipathy*, I have learned the value of paying great attention to detail. It was a harsh lesson learned, and one I shall not soon forget," said Daa'Shond. His dead-black eyes showed not a flicker of emotion, though his ice-cold facial expression and cruel, twisted, slit-mouth made his silently seething rage perfectly clear. "In the interests of transparency, I must inform you that the voice you just heard was that of Azvoc, a warrior of the planet that was thought dead... *Feer'aal*. I trust the address to your fellow warriors was well-received, Azvoc?

"We will hold the gathering in the coming hours. I am confident of a positive outcome," said Azvoc in typical Ferrucian fashion: blunt and cold.

"Excellent," Daa'Shond exclaimed, "The Gantuans also listen in as we speak. I'm sure you can understand their apprehension, particularly after the atrocities committed against them on Mora by the New Unity." Daa'Shond redirected his narrative to the Gantuan's, "I trust in the sheer weight and nature of the alliance we have formed here. I hope that, after hearing the powerful intent and commitment to ending our common enemy, this will sway your decision to join us, Gantuan brothers?" said Daa'Shond, using his most persuasive tone. A non-committal, gutterral grunt and snort was the curt response from the Gantuan's.

"Pah! Get back to us, mwah!" added Daa'Shond, in an attempt to conceal his glaringly-obvious embarrassment. He cut the Gantuan's comm feed and addressed his allies.

"Forget those slow-witted oafs, we do not need them. We are strong. Meet me here in two cycles; I look forward to hosting you, we have much to plan." With his closing sentence, Daa'Shond cut the feed, and spun in his chair to face Kan Vok Tah's ex employees.

"As your new boss, the first task I entrust you with - is to make this place ready for our guests… Oh, and ensure you are well-rested and sharp, should they bring any trouble with them… But firstly, fetch me a warm, spiced Raktee. Mwah!!"

"I'm not sure putting up with *him* is worth any amount of money," said one of the muscle-bound beings, sighing to himself as he followed Daa'Shond's orders.

Chapter Three

A Mission

"Hello old friend," said Tecta, placing his hand warmly on Greem's shoulder, "We would request an audience with Vrin, if now is a good time."

"Greetings friends. Vrin is older than I have seen her in a very long time," was Greem Tah's concerned reply. It was followed by a deep sigh, "Come, she's through here." Greem gestured to a doorway.

"Vrin, we have visitors," said Greem Greem Tah cheerily.

"I know, I invited them. They just don't know that yet," Vrin replied, "Tecta, Pilot. Greetings, my dear friends. I have been waiting for you to come to our door."
Tecta and Pilot were taken aback by Vrin's appearance. She looked ancient… dark, sunken eyes, white hair and withered skin. Her bony fingers resembled brittle talons… so frail. Vrin was the gauge; subjected to the endless yoyo-ing in her age, as the balance of power in the galaxy shifted back and forth from light to dark, and so on. It wasn't so long ago that she had appeared as a fresh-faced young adult, barely out of her teens. Peace and war came and went, but Vrin endured… it was her destiny to do so.

"Before you say anything, the feelings and fears that brought you here are not unfounded, my old friend. A great threat rises, and those nagging feelings of yours are a credit to you. I was so sure things were going to be different this time. We've had an extended period of peace, and I dared to dream that I could finally find a balance, and live some semblance of a 'normal' life. But then merely days ago, the aging took hold once more, and so savagely, that I began to believe that I might meet my final end," said Vrin, with a look of shame, "Then, the realisation hit me. If my life ended, everything I know and love would be beyond saving. The galaxy would be lost to darkness. I was reminded of my true purpose here. This new threat; it already spreads… and I fear as do you, that we don't currently have the means to stop it. Tecta, we need to seek advice from a source far more ancient than either you or I." Vrin paused, looking reflective.

"You don't need to feel ~~no~~ any shame Vrin," said Tecta, empathising wholeheartedly. After all, it wasn't so long ago that he himself had tried to end his own existence, with his self-imposed exile. "What is this source you speak of?"

"The Prophetic Head," said Vrin, with complete sincerity.

"Pardon my bluntness, but, the Prophetic Head is a myth!" sneered Tecta.

"It wasn't that long ago that no one believed you really existed my friend," said Vrin, "The galaxy has changed much since the coming of the Children, and the activation of the Unity Spire. Many things thought to be myth and legend have been proven true, not least of all the re-emergence of the sentient planets. Surely you know better than to dismiss the Head as a fable," smiled Vrin, "Besides, he's an old friend."

"You know him?" Tecta's surprise was impossible to hide, "Because in all my years of existence, I have neither seen nor heard any evidence of such an enduring being, until now. We will seek out this being and request his council. It is no lie that you have been right about such matters before, on more than one previous occasion," said Tecta.

"You must go immediately my friends, you have a long journey *ahead*, excuse the pun," said Vrin, with a familiar twinkle in her aged eyes. Pilot, who had been unusually quiet for some time, couldn't contain himself, and burst out in uncontrollable laughter.

"Dis good one friend Vrin, you say ahead, we go see da Head." Pilot continued to laugh for an uncomfortably long time. Vrin smiled at Pilot's good-natured sense of humour. "Friend Vrin, you look not as old now. How dis?"

"Hope, my friend - you two have provided us with hope." And it was true… she had clearly started to de-age once more.

"Come Pilot, we have much to do." Tecta shook his head at his companion, and bid farewell to Vrin.

"Ahead," said Pilot, still chuckling to himself. As Greem showed them to the door, he paused before opening it.

"There's one more thing Tecta. I have something for you, please take this." Greem handed Tecta a fob, and an odd-looking device, "This tracker will locate the Prophetic Head's whereabouts," said Greem.

"And this?" asked Tecta, holding up the

fob.

"That fob will grant you control of my starship, *The Nomad*. Vrin seems to believe that you will be returning with others. *The Nomad* is large enough to serve as a transport; she's also very, very fast, and has a fully-equipped weapons array - should you run into any trouble." Greem placed his hand on Tecta's upper arm, "Go safely my friends, and may you return with some much-needed help and answers."

"Thank you Greem, we will succeed," said Tecta solemnly.

"We be care with ship friend. Pilot good pilot. You no worry, okay."

Chapter Four

The Cult of Rarvin

Kraqtar Ravine Cave System: The Planet Feer'aal

Feer'aal was stuck in the dark ages. The Ferrucians were so obsessed with war, that when no one else would fight them, they started to fight each other. Thinning their own population with the infighting, the few that remained called for a truce, and later formed the Cult of Rarvin.

"Brothers and Sisters, it is time for Feer'aal to rise. We must begin the fight to regain our true status in the galaxy," said Azvoc, the leader of the Cult of Rarvin.

"Like-minded others have reached out to us, in the hope that we would be agreeable to forming a powerful alliance to bring down the New Unity!"

"The Cult of Rarvin follows only the word of Rarvin himself. We do not make alliances!" Vaksh predictably protested.

"Vaksh, your memory is short. Do you not remember studying the history of the dark reign of Rarvin?" Azvoc asked.

"I remember it well Azvoc, and those alliances failed. The Slaavene betrayed him, and the Raktarians were more interested in their inventions than taking action." Vaksh loved nothing better than being disagreeable.

"I am telling you that I mean to go with or without you. I will not sit here forever taking blind pot-shots at any unusual readings in Feruccian space, waiting for something to happen. I will make things happen. Whether you join me or not is your choice. We are too few in number to achieve this alone." Azvoc had a plan, and he would stick to it, even if it meant moving against the Cult. He believed, unwaveringly, that this is what Rarvin himself would have done. Azvoc knew, in his heart of hearts, that the Cult would never choose to follow Vaksh over him. Vaksh was a cruel, callous creature, with a toxic attitude. He was bitterly jealous of Azvoc, and his popularity among the other members of the Cult.

"You presume to know the workings of the mind of Rarvin?" An unfamiliar voice boomed and echoed around the cave. The accusing words carried threat and violence.

"Who are you? How and why are you here?" Vaksh spat his questions aggressively at their uninvited guest. *Shhiing*, a blade flashed from the darkness, slicing Vaksh from hip to shoulder. The precise strike passed clean through muscle, bone and Vaksh's dark heart. He lay in two pieces on the cold stone floor, blood and gore sprawling around him. The gathered Feruccians stood stunned into silence. As shocking and brutal as this sudden attack was, Azvoc could only think about one thing; not retaliation or vengeance for the fallen Vaksh, but the form of attack that the stranger had used, and the nature of the weapon he had used to deliver it. He recognised it as the Ma'Kra, an ancient combat style of *Feer'aal*. Very few had ever heard of it: even fewer had ever learned how to use it.

"How do you know the Ma'Kra? You are not even from Feer'aal! And how do you come to have the Feruccian Blade of Ancients in your possession? Only one has wielded that weapon in our modern history…" Azvoc demanded an explanation.

"In order for you to fully understand, I will need to start at the beginning," the stranger replied, "Firstly, I do not apologise for killing your clansman. I need you to understand the nature of what I am. A statement had to be made."

"Well, you clearly achieved your first goal," said Azvoc.

"If you truly worship Rarvin, you will want to hear what I have to tell," the stranger replied. Azvoc looked at the gathered, silently seeking their approval to let the stranger speak. The consensus was clear from their nods and gestures.

"We will hear what you have to say," Azvoc eventually replied.

"Has Feruccian hospitality really fallen this far?" said the stranger, with a disappointed shake of his head.

"It has been a long time since we have had 'visitors'. This way. So that we may sit," said Azvoc, gesturing to a small stone circle.

"You may all sit, I prefer to stand as I deliver my story to you." The gathered Feruccians eased themselves down to the ground. They dared not to take their eyes off the strangely formidable man, who now stood upon the tallest rock of the speaking circle. Clad in pristine, Feruccian, military uniform, he silently commanded the attention of the room.

"This body that you see before you, once belonged to a noble being named Kalto," the stranger began.

"What do you mean *used to belong to*?" asked Azvoc, tentatively.

"Patience!" the stranger hissed, "As I have said. I must start from the beginning."

"Please continue," said Azvoc. No one had ever witnessed such subservience from Azvoc - this stranger carried a genuine air of superiority.

"Kalto was a simple scavenger. He had but one purpose in life: to avenge the death of his childhood friend Shrimp. After years of frustration and endless torment, his chance finally presented itself, in the dying moments of the Battle of Mora. He meant to destroy the wicked tyrant, Injis. She was already close to death, buried under a mass of white rock, only her head visible. Kalto was poised to strike the final blow, holding a boulder aloft. He meant to obliterate her vile skull. However, it wasn't to be - he was denied his vengeance by two Protector Droids. They demanded he desist or face death. Injis was to be dealt with by her own people. It crossed Kalto's mind to carry out his vengeance regardless. However, he knew Shrimp wouldn't want it to end this way. In that moment, Kalto realised that there was another far more cruel and tormenting way to exact his vengeance on Injis. He knelt beside her, and whispered into her ear. He promised her that Shrimp would be avenged, that he would find her cohort Vrex, and end him, so that her legacy could never come to be. This single act was to be his last and biggest mistake. As Kalto leaned in towards Injis, he unwittingly received a parting gift from her. The black smoke, (the essence of The Hushed), that had corrupted her for so long, stealthily exited her dying body and infiltrated Kalto through his respiratory system. From that day onwards, his mind and body were not his own. He was plagued by visions, drowned by voices, and suffered long bouts of amnesia. He was lost. His life no longer felt like it had any meaning. His single-minded quest for vengeance had been his driving force, his reason to be, for so very long.

Over time, Kalto was weakened. He'd become directionless, mentally unstable. He had all but abandoned the idea of killing Vrex - his search for him had been fruitless. Eventually, his mind failed him. His consciousness faded away… to leave only the shell that was his body. The black smoke had broken him down from the inside. It spread throughout his entire being like an aggressive virus, evolving… mutating… (creates more tension and suspense here) and now it existed outside of the Phase Realm, without the need for mind invasion or mirror hosts. *The Hushed* had, for the first time in their existence, become a stable presence in the Physical Realm. They provided my consciousness with a way back. Kalto is no more. I am Rarvin, the keeper of *The Essence*, and I have returned to lead my people." He held the Blade of Ancients aloft and roared, "Are you with me?" Azvoc rose to his feet, and bowed his head in respect. He wholeheartedly believed every word the stranger had spoken, and he was not alone in his belief, as the gathered Feruccians followed suit, and began the chant "Rarvin Cha, Rarvin Cha, Rarvin

Cha!"

Rarvin stepped down from his pedestal to welcome the embraces of his people. When Azvoc stepped up to embrace him, Rarvin spoke again.

"Azvoc, you will be my right-hand in our return to glory. Come, we must plan for what lies ahead. Tell me more of this alliance that you were speaking of upon my arrival."

"It was a means to an end; our numbers are few, but now it feels more like an opportunity for domination," said Azvok. He smiled a dry, emotionless smile - a smile that was far removed from the intent of the words that he spoke.

"Then we must take that opportunity," replied Rarvin.

Chapter Five

Treelo

It had been two days since *Won'Kaat Station* had been placed on a tokenistic lockdown. The scant security detail, (which was in fact nothing more than a bunch of low-lifes taking backhanders,) had to at least look like they were taking some form of action. Not that anyone actually cared enough to investigate the murder of Kan Vok Tah. To pass the time, Treelo indulged himself in the 'legendary' Shrabesque - that could only be found in the small diner in the square. Greem Greem Tah had told Treelo it was a traditional recipe - the likes of which he had never tasted anywhere else. Treelo had certainly never tasted anything quite like it… but not in a good way. He was glad of the warm, spiced Raktee to chase the flavour away. He watched the comings and goings of the station's inhabitants; including the Pleasure Bots, (who had scared the life out of Pilot on his last visit), just before the activation of the Unity Spire. He couldn't help but chuckle to himself at the memory of Pilot's face when he had told him of his encounter with a Pleasure Bot. Pilots were such innocent, unassuming people, yet so naturally wise and resourceful. Ever since Pilot was named as the Sixth Child of the New Unity, the two of them had had little opportunity to spend much time together, and

Treelo missed his friend. It was a feeling
that was most unexpected and alien to him.
Maybe he truly had changed, and was no longer
the lone wolf - he now longed for his pack.
Had he committed his last reckless, albeit
noble, act?

His cosy train of thought was interrupted by a
sight that he almost refused to believe. A
Feruccian warrior, impeccably dressed in full,
formal, battle garb strode, head held high,
through the crowded walkways. Although none of
the locals had even so much as batted an
eyelid at him, Treelo's curiosity had got the
better of him. He couldn't help himself. Tecta
had, for all intents and purposes, ended
Feer'aal. Its people were few in number, and
their technology had been all but decimated.
He needed to know who this warrior was, and
why he was here. He placed payment for his
'meal' on the battered old dining table, and
set off after the fearsome-looking
individual. After a few moments following at a
safe distance, he saw another conspicuous-
looking character - darting too and fro
amongst the crowds of the station. It was the
strange creature who had approached him in Kan
Vok's bar, Daa'Shond. Treelo remembered his
face and name, on account of them both being
so unusual. Daa'Shond seemed to be gesturing
to the Feruccian to follow him. Treelo
continued to stalk them along the main
thoroughfare. The pair rounded the corner that
led to the drug, drink and gambling district.
He hung back, and watched as Daa'Shond entered
Sin, (the establishment that formerly belonged
to Kan Vok Tah), and was followed by the
Feruccian warrior. The door slammed firmly
shut behind them. Kan Vok's former associates

stood guard outside. *At least they'd swiftly found new, gainful employment,* he thought. However, the bar was clearly not open for business.

A sudden commotion caught Treelo's attention. The crowds that milled about the gambling district split, and a shabbily-dressed giant of a man reeled backwards out of the crowd, slamming hard into a support column, before slumping heavily to the ground. A tall, thick-set, robed figure emerged from the crowd. The figure was flanked by more Feruccian warriors. It appeared as if they were the robed figure's security detail. As the group approached Sin, Kan Vok's former associates stepped forwards to intercept them. They were struck down before they could utter a word, sliced and diced by multiple Feruccian blades. The tall, robed figure casually kicked away the cubed chunks of torso, and entered the building with his cohorts filing in behind him, spitting on their victim's remains as they went.

Treelo needed to know what was going on inside Sin - this was far too tantalising a situation to simply walk away from. *There must be another way in,* he thought, as he scanned the building's façade. But then again, he didn't really want to be inside that nest of psychopaths, and *so much* for *not returning to the scene of his crime. The old impulsive Treelo was still in there somewhere.* His thoughts caused him to smile, but it soon faded, when he realised that this was no use - there was only one way in and out. He wasn't about to go toe-to-toe with Feruccian warriors either.

There's more than one way to skin a Voxen, he said out loud. He found one of the many shady alcoves that were abundant on the station, and activated his combat suit's data-pad. It had been a while, but he was going to have to dust off the hacking skills he'd acquired in his misspent youth. Firstly, he sent a narrow particle band communication to Unity, not the most reliable method of communication, but it was virtually untraceable. The New Unity needed to know about the events that were unfolding here, and plan accordingly.

Treelo went to work, turning his full attention to accessing the security cameras inside Sin. Annoyingly, the visual feeds were too heavily encrypted for him to access without being noticed. The only thing he could access was an audio feed, laced with static interference, but it would have to do...

Chapter Six

The Essence

Azvoc drew a plain glass vial from his pocket and placed it in the centre of the gambling table. A black, smoky substance swirled hypnotically inside the small vessel. Vrex, Daa'shond and Son Reynar regarded it with indifference.

"This is what you bring to us? Just another narcotic?!" Daa'Shond was extremely underwhelmed by Azvoc's offering.

"This is far from anything that simple," said Azvoc, "I have the living host of this substance here with me. Would you permit him to join us?"

"The host? Fine!" snapped Daa'Shond, "But you should be warned. I am not impressed thus far."

"Rarvin!" Azvoc called, "Please enter." Rarvin, in his formidable new body, strode confidently into the room.

"Rarvin? Is he named after the failed supreme warrior of Feer'aal?" sniped Vrex, who still stared at the vial to see if he was missing something.

"Thank you," said Rarvin in deep, silken tones.

"For what?" asked Vrex, cockily.

"For giving me an excuse," Rarvin replied casually.

"What do you mean by that?" asked Vrex. He looked up and saw Rarvin for the first time since he had entered the room. His arrogance was instantly quashed, replaced by a countenance of shock and terror. He recognised the man that towered over him. The atmosphere of the room had changed completely - it was now one of awe and uncertainty.

"Kalto!" Vrex exclaimed, "How?"

"The former inhabitant of this body found you truly abhorrent, and this is the least I can do to repay him for my second chance."

"W-w-what is?" said Vrex, with utter panic in his voice. He was on his feet, backing away from the approaching Rarvin. "What are you doing?"

"There is nothing to be gained from running, your fate is inevitable. You are to become the first exhibit of my new collection." Vrex knew only too well what Rarvin meant by his 'collection'. He had heard the tales of Rarvin's trophy room, the place where he'd kept the stuffed corpses of his enemies, and even his own family! All of them were slain and went through the process of taxidermy by his own hand. Vrex had lost any semblance of calm. There was a distinct lack of fight in his eyes… he knew his time was up…

In a flash, Rarvin unsheathed a dagger and plunged it through Vrex's throat, pinning him to the wall. Blood gurgled and rose up to spill from his gaping mouth, painting his contorted lips crimson. His eyes were fixed wide-open in terror. Rarvin approached Vrex and stared into those eyes with deep, cold, intent. When the light within had almost faded, Rarvin steadily exhaled, releasing *The Essence*… it disappeared into Vrex's nostrils like smoke up twin flues.

Rarvin turned to look at the stunned faces of those gathered round the table.

"Now the fun's over, where were we?" said Daa'Shond, feigning indifference. His black eyes glistened as a ferocious smile lit up his grotesque features.

"Oh, the fun has only just begun," said Rarvin, as he took Vrex's seat at the table.

A gurgling sound came from behind Rarvin. At first it was barely audible, but swiftly grew in volume, until it culminated in a sharp, breathy, gasp.

"Miraculous, it gets me every time," chirped Rarvin, "Now, tell my friends who you are." His voice now carried an authoritative timbre.

"*We are The Essence.*" Chilling, over-lapping voices hissed from Vrex's impaled body. They ranged from guttural booming to thin, rasping whispers, interspersed with occasional gasps and broken words - the latter of which was a bi-product of the throat trauma Rarvin's blade had inflicted.

"What is your purpose?" Rarvin asked.

"*Your will is our purpose,*" The Essence replied.

"What is it?" asked Daa'Shond, intrigued.

"They are able to exist in a similar manner to myself. They are loyal, obedient and unscrupulously violent weapons. They are remarkable, but in the most basic terms, they are murderous drones. I am the only victim of *The Hushed* whose consciousness has returned fully and taken ownership of its host. Some have achieved occasional clarity of thought, but could not sustain it. *The Essence* will make a formidable army, but I need commanders, thinkers, who are as driven as I. That is where you three come in," he addressed Daa'Shond, Azvoc and Son Reynar.

The roles of those gathered within the room had changed significantly since Rarvin's savage entrance. He had become the leader, and Daa'Shond wasn't stupid enough to challenge him. He would play the role that had been forced upon him.

"I assume there is a plan then?" Daa'Shond asked.

"Of course, and a deliciously vile plan it is too. Firstly, I need a volunteer to carry out a test mission to measure the scale of what *The Essence* can achieve. I will give you a moment to digest what you have just witnessed, then we will talk. Come Azvoc, let us partake in some refreshment," said Rarvin, as he exited the room and headed to the bar.

"Are you really going to start a new *collection?* whispered Azvoc, as they walked.

"Of course not, that's so last incarnation," Rarvin replied, showing a rare flash of humour, "We need to be single-minded in our mission, focused and without such distraction."

* * * * * * * * *

Daa'Shond gave it a few moments, then boldly followed them into the bar. Son Reynar hung back cautiously. He had the distinct feeling that he needed to distance himself from Daa'Shond, or Rarvin would look upon him with the same disdain.

"So, what is your grand plan Rarvin?"

Daa'Shond's snide tone tailed off, as he regarded the Feruccian warriors that lined the walls of the establishment, "Who are your friends?" he continued.

"Patience...they are none of your concern, and… can you not take a moment to appreciate the enormity of what you have just witnessed in that room?" sighed Rarvin.

"Oh, your display was disturbingly impressive, we are just eager to set plans in motion...aren't we Reynar," snivelled Daa'Shond, looking for some show of solidarity from the Raktarian. It never came.

Daa'Shond fidgeted nervously.

"What's more...I would like to know how you plan to control those things, when they turn like Vrex in there.' Daa'Shond gestured to the doorway behind him. Rarvin glared at Daa'Shond, his eyes filled with irritation.

"The black smoke is a highly-addictive substance. They will follow and obey whoever holds *The Essence*. Drip-feeding is the key to keeping them under control, like rewarding a Voxhund for obeying a command." Rarvin grew bored of explaining.

"And what is our, sorry, your next move?" asked Daa'Shond.

"Fine!" snapped Rarvin, "It will be far simpler to show you than to explain it. Azvoc, prepare the vessel for infusion."

"My pleasure Rarvin." Azvoc disappeared, leaving Daa'Shond to eye Rarvin uncomfortably. He knew that he was way, way out of his depth, yet he also understood the necessity to feign some semblance of control. Azvoc returned with a plain chrome canister. He removed a panel from the wall, and casually connected the canister to the station's ventilation system.

"What is this?" asked Daa'Shond.

"First, we flood the station with a scentless, semi-deadly poison," said Rarvin.

"Then?" asked Daa'Shond.

"This will leave them all at the brink of death. Then I will unleash *The Essence* into the station."

"And then?"

"We wait," was Rarvin's stunted response.

"What? We'll be infected too!" snapped Daa'Shond, "I didn't sign up for this!" he protested.

"Calm your cowardly nerves Daa'Shond. Take these and pass one to Son Reynar." Rarvin handed a pair of auto-injectors to Daa'Shond, who received them with trembling digits, "Press it against your neck, and you will become immune to the effects of *The Essence*," said Rarvin.

"I offer you my most humble thanks, Lord Rarvin… um, forgive me for asking but, how long does it last?" snivelled Daa'Shond.

"It is a permanent solution," said Rarvin, waving Daa'Shond's apologies away, "The enduring memories of the victims of *The Hushed* will flood the bodies and minds of every sentient being upon this station."

"Those outside of this room, and those who have not been afforded the protection of this inoculation from our glorious leader, of course," said Daa'Shond, seeking extra reassurance.

"Indeed. Once inhaled, *The Essence* will amplify the host's darkest desires, and awaken the murderous impulses that all living beings harbour deep inside themselves. *The Essence*, with the strongest of wills, may wake with self-awareness - in total control of their new host bodies - as I myself did. They will be terminated."

"What! Why?" questioned Daa'Shond.

"We already have our generals. Unless you wish one of them to take your place?" snapped Rarvin.

"Sorry," Daa'Shond mumbled, apologising in simpering tones.

"All other hosts will be transformed into vicious drones, filled with myriad memories, dark experiences and impulses, much like our dearly-departed friend Vrex." Rarvin gestured to the room where Vrex's bloodied corpse still hung from the wall, "They will be our primary weapon, obedient and selfless in their execution of our plan. They will spread *The Essence* far and wide, to every planet of this New Unity, and far beyond, until we control the entire galaxy."

* * * * * * * * *

Treelo listened open-mouthed to the broken, static-filled audio feed. He could barely believe what he was hearing. His heart was beating out of his chest. He needed to get somewhere safe, however he was acutely aware that this was *Won'Kaat Station*, and *safe* wasn't a word this place knew or respected. He'd never make it to his ship, as the docks were on lockdown. His mind raced with questions and the adrenaline associated with sheer panic. *Was this the universe exacting some kind of cosmic revenge on him for murdering Kan Vok Tah?* In a fleeting moment of clarity, Treelo engaged his Tek Shield, to protect himself from the poison filling the station. The steady flow of oxygen inside his combat suit provided a much-needed calming effect. He pulled the loose-fitting hood of his robe over his head, to disguise the facial shielding of the Tek - and not a moment too soon.

A thick black smog spewed from the life support vents, filling the atmosphere of the station with the chokingly-acrid *Essence*. The fog was so dense that everything was plunged into utter darkness. Treelo could see nothing, and all he could hear was the sound of his own panicked breathing inside his mask. He activated the body torches on his combat suit, and tried to orientate himself. He was trying his hardest to breathe through the intense feelings of claustrophobia that threatened to consume him. The ground was littered with choking bodies, but he didn't have time to consider them - he visualised them as an uneven, spongy terrain as he ran over the top of them, as fast as his quivering legs would allow. Something was changing in the atmosphere around him... *The Essence* was thinning, and the bodies beneath him were beginning to move. Their jarring movements were accompanied by snarls, hisses and spitting. Threatening whispers and shrieks filled the air, as *The Essence* roused their new host bodies from their brief slumber.

Treelo, you idiot! He activated the Anti-Grav function on his suit in the nick of time. He rose up through *The Essence* as the possessed hosts clawed and snapped at him with hateful venom, screaming in frustration as he rose up, avoiding their grasp by the slimmest of margins.

Something caught Treelo's eye. Amid the chaos, one creature stood statuesque, eyes trained

solely on him. It appeared to track his every
move. This one was different, composed and
self-aware… an intelligence lit up its clear
eyes. It wasn't rabid or chaotic, but it was
clearly of the same dark ilk. The horde were
completely indifferent to its presence. Treelo
needed to find refuge, so he made a snap
decision to head down to the original sectors
of the station, which was the smart choice.
There were hangers and discarded craft down
there, with numerous hiding spots. He allowed
himself a brief smile - he still had *it* - that
survivor's instinct.

* * * * * * * * * *

What Reynar said next was the last thing
Daa'Shond had expected.
    "I volunteer. I'll take the test mission,"
said Reynar. Daa'Shond was aghast - his only
hope of an ally was abandoning him.
    "Such decisiveness, it's extremely
refreshing," smiled Rarvin, as he signalled
towards two impressive-looking Feruccian
warriors, "Krax and Vardra here will accompany
you and instruct you in the art of herding.
The Essence hosts need to be stowed in your
ship's cargo hold. I trust you have a test
site in mind, given your local knowledge of
this system?"
    "Believe me, I know the perfect place. I
thank you for this opportunity and this
formidable weapon," Reynar responded, taking
his leave.
    "Krax," said Rarvin.
    "Sir," was the curt reply Krax gave, as he
turned to face his leader.
    "You need not restock the hold of my ship.
It is already filled with something very

special."

"Understood Sir." Krax gave the Feruccian salute, then exited the bar to join Reynar.

Rarvin turned his attention towards his other two generals.

"Once we have affirmation of the effectiveness of *The Essence* on a planetary scale, we will execute the next phase of our plan. Daa'Shond, you and I will go to *Veela VI*. Azvoc, you will take *Mora* - then, once we have allowed them to witness the death of their idealistic false utopia, together we will take their hub of operations: the planet *Unity*."

"Rarvin, will you not be accompanying me to Mora?" asked Azvoc.

"No, you have my full confidence. Take the remainder of the warrior detail with you and lead *The Essence* new-borns to your ship, in preparation for my order. There is an irksome presence hiding aboard this station. I will find it and deal with it. Then I will take Daa'Shond with me to *Veela VI*. Once we have taken the planet, we will rendezvous with you at the edge of Unity Space, to exact our final vengeance," snarled Rarvin, clearly irritated that any being had escaped *The Essence*.

"What happened to no distractions," smiled Azvoc.

"This is different, it's sport," said Rarvin dryly.

"As you wish Rarvin. Warriors, with me!" said Azvoc, leading the Feruccians from the room.

"Am I not trusted to complete my own mission Rarvin?" asked Daa'Shond, spikily.

"Very insightful," was Rarvin's cold response. He removed his weapons and placed them on the table in front of Daa'Shond, "Wait here, this shouldn't take long."

"Won't you need your weapons?" asked Daa'Shond, clearly confused.

"I have everything I need right here." He pounded his chest with his fist, "As I have said, this is sport, and in the spirit of fairness, certain rules must be observed. Contrary to popular belief, I am not a complete savage." Rarvin's face was full of cold intent and menace. He left the bar - the solid metal doors sealing silently behind him. Rarvin pulled up his hood and merged seamlessly into *The Essence* hosts. He expelled intermittent bursts of the black smoke as he walked - to keep *The Essence* close enough to conceal his presence. He needed to think like the mortal, linear being he once was. They were irrational and prone to doing exactly the wrong thing. It was a simple choice between scouring the very top of the station, or descending way down to the basement levels. They always went to extremes - especially when they were running scared.

* * * * * * * * *

Suddenly, Daa'Shond was alone with his nagging doubts… he was seriously out of his depth. Rarvin had derailed his plans, and Daa'Shond was far from where he wanted to be. He was supposed to be running the show, pulling the strings. He thought briefly about running and relocating somewhere remote. But Rarvin had a long reach, and there were too many sets of treacherous eyes in the galaxy that would willingly give him up. In truth, Daa'Shond was

too much of a coward to risk being caught, and
the thought of Rarvin's retribution was
terrifying. He was in too deep… he knew he was
going to have to see this through to its
grisly conclusion.

Chapter Seven

The Return Of Son Reynar

A Raktarian freighter was a rare sight in these times. It was a bold symbol of wealth and prosperity, from a planet and people that had cut themselves off from the rest of the solar system. The immaculately-polished hull and beautiful attention to every last detail was outstanding. Such pride in engineering had been absent from Unity Space for decades; replaced by Junkers, fighters built from mis-matched salvage, pirate ships, and all manner of cobbled-together, barely-space-faring craft. To be seeing this sight must have meant a mission of utmost importance to Raktar was in the offing. However, the glorious facade of this ship belied the truth of the horrors that inhabited its cargo hold.

Son Reynar sat alone on the flight deck of the impressive cruiser. He painted a picture of reflective solitude, staring down at his mechanical hand as he flexed his fingers and thumb. The Raktarian technology melded seamlessly with his biological limbs. His thoughts drifted back to the beginning of this journey, to the recovery he had embarked upon to arrive at this point...

From his perspective, Taire had betrayed and cheated him. He'd left him trapped and alone,

deep within that snow-covered plateau on
Raktar. The memories of those events were
crystal- clear. The dark and perilous cold…
where the only sounds had been the whipping of
the wind, and the desperate howls and low
growling of the predatory Ice Voxen… circling
the entrance to the pit high above him, in
desperate need of a feed. These creatures
could smell blood from a thousand metres away,
and on closer inspection, they could sense
when something injured and edible was close.
Climbing out of that deep hole hadn't been an
option, (not only had Reynar been missing a
hand and a foot after his confrontation with
Taire), even if he could have made the climb,
he wasn't foolish enough at the time to have
taken on a pack of Ice Voxen, when he was in
~~his~~ that awful condition. There had only been
one course of action available to him. He had
to wait it out. He remembered activating a
distress beacon, and deploying a Cryo-gel
Cocoon to preserve himself. It was an
ingenious yet relatively untested technology,
but he had had no choice but to risk it… A
singular emotion filled Reynar's entire being.
Not fear, or panic; but unadulterated rage. A
burning anger was fuelled by his lust for
vengeance. Reynar had made himself a promise.
He would get out of this darkness, find Taire,
and destroy him.

When Reynar had volunteered for Rarvin's test
mission and had been gifted *The Essence*, he
knew the time to exact his vengeance had come.
~~and~~ The mere thought of it was scintillating,
all consuming. His mind raced, fantasizing
about the endless ways that he could inflict
pain and suffering on his nemesis.
        "TAIRE, I'M COMING FOR YOU!" he shouted

maniacally, littering his lips with spittle.

Chapter Eight

Shinara Prime

It had been a little while since the news broke of Pilot's celebration, and the mood amongst the crew of *The Seeker* continued to be one filled with excitement. The pending celebrations were to be held on *Veela VI*. The crew were overwhelmed with joy for Pilot. He was a most deserving recipient of this honour, and it needed to be marked. Well, the whole crew except Runt, who still refused to recognise his heritage as a member of the Pilot race. It was a rare and awful thing to see a lifeform of such diminutive stature - having the ability to hold such a vast amount of resentment.

Taire and the rest of the crew were not only excited for the celebrations, they were also keen to see for themselves the progress that had been made on *Veela VI* since Tam's re-enlivening of the planet. Besides that, it had been an age since any of them had had a vacation of any kind. They knew however, that they needed to stay on their guard and complete their current mission. The routine sweep they embarked upon was to serve as a message to any potential antagonists that the New Unity was always present, and that they were not getting sloppy or complacent in any way, shape or form.

The mirthful chuntering of the crew filled the bridge. The exhilarating sound of high spirits, rare and refreshing as it was, was cut abruptly short by the shrill pinging of an alarm.

"Taire, our sensors have picked up a signal," said Sanvar.

"What kind of signal?" Taire asked.

"It appears to be a call for help... though it could just be an old signal - it's not one that I recognise, and there's no signature embedded. It's originating from the surface of *Shinara Prime*," Sanvar replied.

"Runt, scan for life signs in the proximity of the signal," commanded Taire.

"Runt do scan already, no, no life no."

"We should investigate, just in case. Sanvar, take us down. Runt, continue scanning, and let me know if you pick anything up."

"No problem," said Sanvar.

"Same," said Runt.

"You can't help yourself, can you Taire? But I do love it when you're authoritative," laughed Nel.

"Blunkt brapt," chirped Clint - his equivalent of scoffing at Nel's comment.

Taire was too intrigued to even comment. His interest had been piqued by the distress signal. He stood staring intently at the planet below, as *The Seeker* entered *Shinara Prime's* upper atmosphere. The planet was largely uninhabited since *The Hushed's* original mind invasion. It was quite possibly the most successful, unaided assault in their reign of terror. The entire population had fallen prey to the mind invasion and murdered their own families, friends and neighbours. It

was a self-inflicted genocide, commanded by
the will of *The Hushed*. A sparse scattering of
native wildlife was thought to be all that
remained. Taire found it strange when thinking
back to the attack that had happened - he was
still in hiding on *Veela VI* with Tecta, Lu and
Gliis. Back then, he didn't even know if other
beings still existed in the galaxy, let alone
that he would encounter so many people of
different species, some of whom would become
his crew and closest friends. *The Seeker*
touched gently down on to the dry, crunchy
terrain.

    "The signal is coming from below the
surface," reported Sanvar.
    "Clint and I will go and investigate,"
said Taire, "Nel, stay here with Runt and
Sanvar to guard the ship. Keep an eye on the
scanners - this world is largely unknown to
us."
    "Runt no need babysitter."
    "What are *you* gonna do if someone attacks
the ship? Cute them to death," said Sanvar
with a smirk, "I for one would welcome Nel's
continued presence."
    "Runt more tough than friend think." Runt
was still very wary of Nel, a fact that he
failed to hide with any level of success. Even
though there had been no incidents or any sign
of her systems being corrupted since Taire had
incorporated the Tek into her systems, Runt
continued to harbour serious doubts and
misgivings towards her.
    "My pleasure," said Nel, "...and Runt,
you're welcome too," she said, winking at him
playfully. After the shame had subsided from
being controlled by the Dark Mother, she had
grown in confidence once more, and thankfully

regained an element of her previous swagger and sass. Runt ignored her comment, grumbled something rude, and busied himself with running routine diagnostics on *The Seeker*.

"I *will* win that little Runt over," said Nel, whist smiling at Taire and Clint.

"I have not a single doubt that you will," Taire smiled. Clint bleeped in agreement.

"Clint, stop repeating my words, it's getting tiresome." Taire was mildly agitated with Clint, who gave a blunkt sound in reply. It appeared to be the cybernetic version of blowing a raspberry.

"You two be careful. I don't want anything happening to my boys," said Nel with a gentle smile. She raised her left hand, and Taire raised his right hand to meet it - they dwelled palm-to-palm with eyes locked for a moment.

"Don't worry, we will," said Taire, gently pressing his lips to Nel's forehead. Clint chirped - signalling at Taire to follow as he exited the Seeker, "Clint, your less-than-subtle displays of jealousy are second-to-none."

"Blunkt," Clint replied, aggressively.

The two of them stepped out of the ship, and into the dry air of the alien world of *Shinara Prime*. *The Seeker's* hatch hissed and closed gently behind them. *Shinara Prime* was a desolate, non-threatening place, yet somehow it felt on the cusp of being eerie. Maybe the atmosphere held the memories of the horrors that befell its former inhabitants. It was a strangely beautiful place, with a multitude of unique quirks. Columns of precious rocks populated the surface, their jaunty, extreme angles reflected the sunlight and refracted it

in all directions - it was like a living
palace of ice. The planet's light was
majestic, containing shimmering tones of blue
and violet that painted the landscape. Taire
found himself momentarily lost in the natural
beauty around them. Clint, who was less
enamoured with their new surroundings, made
his way to the edge of an unremarkable opening
in the ground. He gave several bleeps and
chirping sounds. Taire was torn away from his
living daydream by Clint's twittering.

"Is the signal coming from down there?
Best we have a look then," said Taire. Clint
protested briefly, "Come on, don't be a
scaredy droid, we'll be fine. I'll go first."
It was difficult to penetrate the darkness
below them in order to see what lay inside the
opening. Taire engaged the body torches on his
combat suit, and stepped into the opening.

Tecta had insisted that all Children of the
New Unity must wear traditional combat suits
at all times - they were far too important to
take any risks. At this moment, Taire was
thankful that he had followed his mentor's
instructions. The suits' anti-grav thrusters
made Taire's descent much simpler. The light
beams emanating from his combat suit also
illuminated his immediate surroundings very
effectively. Clint entered the chasm, hovering
cautiously behind Taire.

"Clint, do you see anything?" asked Taire.
Clint gave a short, disappointed *Nurgh* sound
for no. Taire hung in the air and began a
slow, three-hundred-and sixty-degree sweep of
the chasm's interior.

"Keep your eyes peeled Clint." The
surveillance sweep was almost complete - when
Clint started blooping excitedly, "Great

work," said Taire.

Far away to their right, a faint, red light pulsed steadily - piercing the darkness that surrounded it. The pair descended gently… and made a soft landing on the cavern floor - right in front of the scarlet distress beacon.

Some proper light would be good about now. No sooner had the thought entered Taire's head, Ve'dow the defence ring gifted to him by the planet Raktar lit up, bathing the cavern with its luminescent green glow.

A deep voice spoke from within the darkness of the cavern, startling them both.
    "I knew that the hero Taire wouldn't be able to resist a good rescue mission." The voice was familiar, smug, and filled with agitation. Taire spun around to face the direction that the voice had come from.
    "Reynar!" exclaimed Taire, trying to hide his shock, "So, you sent the distress call?"
    "I needed to talk privately with your predictable self, and I created an opportunity to do so," Reynar replied.
    "How did you survive that frozen plateau on *Raktar*?" said Taire, still desperately trying to hide his surprise at Reynar being alive.
    "Funny story... actually no; it's not funny at all," said Reynar bluntly, "I truly hate you for what you did to me, as I'm sure you can understand. But, do you know the problem with carrying the burden of so much hatred Taire?"
    "No, I've never been a particularly hateful person," Taire answered.
    "Then let me tell you: it's exhausting. So

how about we put an end to our feud?" said Reynar, extending his hand.

"Your new appendages are nothing short of an artwork," said Taire, distracted by the sight of Reynar's ungloved, cybernetic hand.

"I have heard of many a fetish and quirk, but this is truly niche Taire. If the rumours are true, and you are 'In love' with Nel, then I suppose you might find all forms of artificial tech alluring. I dread to think what you've used that tiny droid for on a lonely night."

"Is that supposed to be some kind of joke?" snapped Taire angrily, "Because it's a strange choice of words considering you are offering a hand in peace. I did what I did to you because I needed to preserve not only my own life, but the whole galaxy. It's regrettable, but I offer no apology for doing my duty." Taire still refused to extend his hand.

"Oh the self-importance," sneered Reynar, "You are not an easy person to make peace with Taire: ever the martyr." Reynar drew a dagger from his belt and sprung a vicious attack, aiming straight at the top of Taire's skull. But Reynar had underestimated Taire; he now had the ability to will the O Blades to do as he wished. He had forged a link with them. They were intuitive, sensing Taire's impulses and actions - sometimes before he was even aware of them himself! With a low hum and whirring sound, Ve'dow met Reynar's attack - stopping it dead mid-swing. Ki'resh flew into Taire's open hand.

"Deceit is not a virtue," said Taire, staring fearlessly into Reynar's hate-filled eyes.

"You should know. You are, after all, the

master of deceit," retorted Reynar, "You
played me to get what you needed, and then
repaid my hospitality with attempted MURDER!"
Reynar roared and launched another
unsuccessful attack.

"Keep telling yourself that if it makes
you feel better," said Taire, stepping away
from his assailant - whilst manually blocking
his third strike with Ve'dow. Reynar's face
contorted in bitter frustration. Taire could
feel Ki'resh pulsing in his hand, eager to
counter-attack, but he was reluctant to
unleash the attack ring.

"Reynar, I do not want to harm you. There
must be a compromise here."

"The feeling is far from mutual," grunted
Reynar, "You hide behind those rings. Allow me
to level the playing field." He now spoke with
pure menace, "I introduce to you, *The
Essence*."

"That sounds like the name of a terrible
musical ensemble," Taire laughed. His mirthful
quip soon dissolved, as the figures of those
hosting *The Essence* emerged from the shadows,
and into Ve'dow's green light. They moved
eerily in stuttering steps, speaking in
barely-audible hissed whispers. Taire felt the
fine hairs of his back stand on end, a shudder
ran the length of his spine. These beings
oozed menace and threat, like a coiled spring
of violence - poised to unfurl in attack at
any second.

"...And you labelled me the master of
deceit," said Taire, You had no intention of
making peace here." He took up a low defensive
stance. The multitude of beings were slowly
advancing upon him. A mixture of many races…
with one thing in common; they were shells

with dead-black eyes. Reynar stepped backwards and laughed mockingly.

"Now Taire, you *will* die…" He turned and walked nonchalantly away, enveloped by the mass of zombie-like beings. Taire powered up his combat suit.

"Clint, get back to the ship now!" Clint protested angrily. "NOW!" Clint reluctantly followed his command.

The menacing sound of *The Essence's* chanted whispers in overlapping voices grew louder. It filled the cavernous space with a thick, disorientating hum. These creatures were not to be reasoned with, they were here with just one intention...to kill. An ear-splitting screech cut through the humming… it was the signal for *The Essence* to attack - their movements became startlingly rapid. Their previous stuttered steps towards him were a ruse; a sly ploy to lull him into thinking time was on his side, that he could just pick them off one-by-one without any urgency. Ve'dow created a defensive force-field around Taire, and he simultaneously unleashed Ki'resh into the onrushing creatures. *The Essence* launched themselves towards him… screaming, kicking and gnashing their teeth like rabid animals. Thick black drool lashed about their grotesque mouths. Ki'resh was cutting them down like a scythe through a crop of reed grass. But for each creature felled, another advanced - like an endless conveyor belt of horror. With each dismemberment came a plume of thick, black smoke which darted around the horde frantically, trying to join with another of the attacking hosts. Several of the plumes headed directly for Taire, but they were repelled by Ve'dow's force-field. Taire equipped the Tek shielding of his combat suit. He wasn't taking any chances, with what was clearly a newly-evolved incarnation of *The Hushed*. These attackers, although different, embodied a chilling familiarity. The feeling of security that the Tek shielding had gifted him was to be a fleeting relief. It was simple mathematics - he was hopelessly outnumbered, and about to be overrun by the seemingly unstoppable wave of these mercilessly-vile creatures.

* * * * * * * * * *

The familiar scream and whine of Nel's weaponry cut through the chaos, sending body parts flailing left, right and centre. Clint followed - spitting laser bolts and electrical charges. He wasn't about to abandon Taire; he had been ordered to go, but Taire hadn't instructed him not to come back. After all, Clint was a very literal life-form.

Far below Nel and Clint, a carpet of writhing bodies covered the cave floor, thrashing and snarling… Taire wasn't even visible. They could only hope that Ve'dow was protecting him somehow, below this hideous mass of pressed flesh. Ki'resh erupted from the sick mess of possessed bodies, illuminating everything with the wash of its whirling green light. The attack ring spun with a wild precision, carving deep into the dense accumulation of bodies from which it had emerged.
    "He's alive!" exclaimed Nel.
    "Blunkt prap braap bip," Clint chimed in, excitedly. Taire was the master of Ki'resh and

Ve'dow. The fact that Ki'resh was still fighting - meant that Taire was still fighting.

Nel deployed her component parts, each a lethal weapon in its own right. With a squelching thud, Nel's weapons rammed into *The Essence*, hacking their way deep into the rabid bodies to reach her beloved Taire.

Far below Nel and Clint's rescue attempt, Taire was using every fibre of his will to keep his breathing steady, fighting the claustrophobia that threatened to send him into a blind panic. He needed to trust the Tek and the O Blades. He hoped desperately that Clint had made it back to *The Seeker*, and that his friends had escaped the horrors that he was now experiencing. Then suddenly, as the blackness thinned before his eyes and the green light of Ve'dow bled through, he felt a rush of momentary relief, before slipping from consciousness. He dared to believe that he was going to make it.

Chapter Nine

Won'Kaat Station

Daa'Shond

Daa'Shond had been waiting in the bar for an entire cycle, although it felt more like a full rotation had passed. He was growing increasingly desperate for Rarvin to return, (something he never thought he would ever even think, let alone admit). He'd drunk himself senseless twice over, accused the clock in the bar of mocking him and lying, and decided that he was going to make a run for it, then talked himself out of it at least twelve times, instead choosing to gorge himself on the entire range of snacks from the bar. He was so utterly terrified, that he didn't even dare to peek outside and see what was going on. He was completely out of distractions when Rarvin's wrist comm chimed; he'd left it behind, along with his weapons.

"Hello, Rarvin's comms, Daa'Shond speaking." Daa'Shond was desperate to hear another voice.

"Oh! It's you, I must speak with Rarvin." Reynar's disappointment was audible.

"He's a little preoccupied right now. He is erm… hunting," Daa'Shond spoke, in hushed tones.

"But I have news for him." Son Reynar's smug voice emanated from Rarvin's comms was all too apparent.

"Is there a message I can pass on?"

"Yes, that it is done. The test planet will soon be encased beneath *The Essence*. The test mission was even more effective than we could have hoped for, and there is more to report."

"Slithering, treacherous scum," Daa'Shond spat off comms, "Oh do tell," sneered Daa'Shond.

"Taire of the New Unity: he and his friends are no more," stated Reynar confidently, "It was almost too easy to lure them in and dispose of them."

"I knew there must be a reason Rarvin favours you over me Reynar. But do not underestimate Taire. We have both previously fallen victim to that false innocence and treachery of his before."

"Oh trust me - he is ended, I saw it myself." Reynar was very ungracious in victory.

"Very well, I will pass this fine news on. What is your next move?" Daa'Shond enquired.

"We are already on our way to the *Slaavene* homeworld." Reynar replied with an air of arrogance.

"Well, that's jolly marvellous. What a clever boy you are. Mwah!!" Daa'Shond ended Reynar's transmission without further comment, he was clearly fishing for higher praise. *Subservient, crawling filth!* squealed Daa'Shond. *I need to be more choosey with future allies.*

"He truly is a monumental arse, isn't he?" Reynar sighed.

"Clearly, but Rarvin knows that already. He will cease to be of any further use soon enough," replied Krax, Reynar's Feruccian escort.

"Well, I just hope I'm there to witness his demise in person," said Reynar, in a spiky, soured tone, "Do we have adequate *Essence* hosts to continue directly to *Slaavene*?"

"We have more than enough in the hold."

"Excellent, they won't know what's hit them."

Chapter Ten

The Death Of A Planet

The Essence spread like a contagion: a chokingly vile epidemic of pure evil engulfing *Shinara Prime*. *The Seeker* burst forth from the darkness, powering up and out through the atmosphere, and cutting a swathe through the swirling waves of matt blackness. Once *The Seeker* had reached the safety of Open Space, Sanvar turned her about, just in time to see the panic- inducing sight that was *The Essence*… eerily creeping across the planet's surface, until it had swallowed every last ray of reflected light. The planet now appeared as a dead, black sphere - hanging still in the vast backdrop of sprawling space. Sanvar deployed a beacon, declaring the planet a no-go area on risk of death. Taire had only barely made it out of that cavern with the help of Nel, and not everyone was lucky enough to have a Nel. The whole crew knew that they were fortunate to have escaped with their lives.

The Seeker hung in a distant orbit in Shinaran Space with her deflated crew, still licking their wounds. Taire had regained consciousness, and the inquest into his uncharacteristically reckless behaviour was underway.

"What good are you to us dead? You are a Child of the Unity: we need you," Nel scorned, although her eyes held a look of relief. Clint chipped in with various rude-sounding bleeps and bloops at every possible opportunity.

"Thanks for the support, *buddy*, you volunteered to come with." He shook his head in mock disappointment.

"Any way, I assume it was *you* who came back for me?" Taire said to Nel.

"See, no friend want babysitter," said Runt. Nel glared at Runt, who simply put his head down and went about his business, if a little awkwardly.

"Damn right it was me! We need you… I need you. Everyone needs you Taire… the whole galaxy," Nel said furiously.

"Ok, okay, I'm sorry. Thank you for coming back for me," conceded Taire, "Although the more pressing matter here is...what are those things… *The Essence?* Why is Son Reynar commanding them?" he added.

"The same Son Reynar we left for dead on *Raktar*?" said Sanvar - the mere mention of that name forced the colour to drain from his face.

"I didn't see this Son Reynar down there," said Nel. At the mention of Reynar's name, Clint gave a low growl. He had seen him, and wanted to stay with Taire to help fight him. "There was nothing except the black smoke and a writhing carpet of rabid bodies when I found you Taire." The foreboding in Nel's tone grew even darker.

"I'm afraid the situation on *Shinara Prime* has escalated, and is actually even worse now," said Nel.

"How can it be any worse?" asked Taire. Sanvar opened the view screen to reveal the matt-black sphere that *Shinara Prime* had become.

"How is this possible?" questioned Taire.

"We didn't hang around to ask questions," said Sanvar, who was still reeling from the revelation that Son Reynar was alive.

"Once we got you out of there, the black smoke rose up from the chasm, and those zombie things, *The Essence* as you call them, surrounded us. They slammed their bodies into the ship - snapping, snarling, and gouging at the metal. Then, as we lifted off, they began to spread: like a wave of tar across the planet's surface," said Nel.

"If they can do this here, then they can do it on inhabited worlds. We need to report this to Unity and declare *Shinara Prime* a no-go zone," said Taire.

"We already have, and you are right in your thinking. We have detected Raktarian cruisers across the system, belonging to the same spec as a ship that our scanners detected leaving orbit during our escape," said Sanvar, "We also reported our findings and sent all the data we have to Unity Command; they advised us to observe and report any further developments, whilst we waited for your condition to stabilise."

"Well, I'm stable, so let's get out of here. We can analyse the surveillance data once we're on our way. If *The Essence* invades any of Unity's worlds - all who inhale that smoke will be turned into one of those things. We need to find a way to stop it. *Veela VI* is the nearest planet to our current coordinates: we need to get there before one of those cruisers does. Runt, open a channel to Lu, they need to know how serious this new threat is."

"Course is set Taire, engaging maximum thrust," said Sanvar. He eased the acceleration matrix forward, and they were on their way.

"Taire, Runt have Miss Nataalu on da comms now," he said proudly.

"Lu, this thing is relentless, and I can't figure a way to stop it. We need a plan and we need it fast. All the data we have has been sent to Unity Command. There are multiple Raktarian cruisers en-route to the home planets, each of which we assume to be carrying *The Essence*, as they call it."

"*The Essence*? Sounds like a bad musical act," Lu replied.

"I know, I said the same thing. But you must listen to me sister...this is no joke. It's bad… really bad. I've never seen a threat of this type, but it's familiar. It is clearly born from *The Hushed*. Advise all citizens to use the Tek. We are headed to *Veela VI* now. I will make contact again when we arrive," said Taire, rushing his words and almost forgetting to breathe.

"I hear you loud and clear Taire. I will consult with the council and alert the home planets. Be safe brother," said Lu.

"You too," Taire replied.

Chapter Eleven

The Disaster Initiative:

Council Hall, Veela VI

Lu acted swiftly upon receiving Taire's message; and called an emergency meeting with Tam, Seventeen and Co-Pilot, (who was acting as Pilot's voice), in his absence. Lu briefed those assembled in the room, relaying Taire's report in fine detail.

"Then it has begun - we have been blind-sided by the enemy," said Seventeen, "What Taire witnessed on *Shinara Prime* is the precursor to what will happen throughout the galaxy. We need to respond immediately."

"What do you suggest, Seventeen? This is unprecedented. How do we defend against this threat?" said Lu, who was fraught with dread.

"We must evacuate the home planets. We have no other option," replied Seventeen, gravely.

"Evacuate them to where? An operation of that scale would take years. It's unheard of." Lu was on the verge of becoming frantic.

"Unheard of - yes, but not unexpected or indeed impossible. *The Nothing* is vast. There is enough space inside," said Seventeen.

"Enough space to accommodate all the citizens of the New Unity?" asked Lu.

"Yes," Seventeen replied, "*The Nothing* is

infinite."

"How will we get them all there?" Lu asked.

"Pilot know dis. Friend Fiddy-Six and friend Tecta make plan long,long,long... time go," said Co-Pilot, in his distinctly croaky tone.

"What plan?" said Lu, with a look of total confusion on her face, "Why didn't I know about any of this?" she snapped angrily.

"Because Tecta needed you to focus on building the New Unity without such distractions, and you have done so, magnificently. We had hoped that this would be nothing more than a precautionary measure," Seventeen answered Lu's question sympathetically. He understood why she was upset.

"Either way," Lu sighed, "I'm glad they did it. Always the Protector above all else." Her bubbling anger began to subside, "So, how do we implement this plan?" she asked.

"Nataalu, I regret that this burden falls upon your shoulders. As leader, you need to address the New Unity and issue the evacuation order. Each planet has modified Loway Pods stowed in *The Silence*, close to each of their cores. Pilots are on their way to the pods as we speak. We are prepared. You must ensure that the evacuations take place. Pilot and Tecta have been tasked with a mission that is critical to all of our futures, so we need to do what we can to keep everyone safe, until they return." Seventeen wasn't entirely comfortable with directing Nataalu, but he had to continue, regardless of his feelings.

"Leader Nataalu. I trust you, as does

Tecta and the Council. I only wish you had as much faith in yourself as we have in you. You can do this, and Tecta would not have left if it wasn't imperative to our collective survival. Even if he knew what was happening here, he couldn't return until his mission was complete."

"I know," she sighed, "It was my suggestion that he had to leave. Though, that was before *The Essence* attacked."

"If he hadn't have gone now, the future we've fought for could be permanently out of our reach. Trust yourself, as we trust you. Tecta asked me to remind you of the words you spoke, should you ever need to hear them. You said you would always do 'whatever is best for them.' Our people need you, now more than ever."

Lu gave a smirk at the reminder, and shook her head.

"Okay Seventeen, we will keep our people safe in *The Nothing* until Tecta returns with some answers, and the hope that we desperately need."

"Remember, you are not alone in this. We are all with you," said Seventeen.

"What I need from you right now Seventeen is for you and your crew to go to *Slaavene*, and support the defence effort/ evacuation."

"But I must protect you in Tecta's absence!" Seventeen protested.

"Tam and I have Protectors here with us, and too many Pilots and Hornets to count. We will organise the evacuation of *Veela VI*."

"As you wish, but I don't like it one bit." Seventeen was less than enthusiastic at the prospect of having to leave Lu and Tam.

"Thirty-Two, I need you to assemble a defensive team and go to *Unity*. The planet has been left sparsely-populated, to allow it time to heal, so the evacuation will be on a much smaller scale. However, it is the home of the Unity Spire, and it must be protected."

"Understood, leader Nataalu. I will prepare my team and leave immediately."

"Gliis and Kee'Pah are already en-route to *Mora*, for another one of their expeditions into *The Silence*. I will brief them of the situation, and ask them to consult with the Order of the White Rock. Their relationship with *Mora* is far more advanced in comparison to us with our own planets - they may have some answers. Go safely, for peace."

"For peace!" The sentiment was echoed by every voice in the room. Nataalu drew a deep breath "Well…" she sighed, *No time like the present*.

"Open all emergency communication channels to the home worlds. It is time to rally the citizens."

* * * * * * * * * *

The galaxy collectively held its breath, as Nataalu appeared on every news feed and public display screen. She took the podium, just like she had done many years before. Only this time, she was the bearer of grim news.

"Citizens of the New Unity. It pains me to bring you this news. Once more we find ourselves under attack. All that we are building, and everything we stand for, make us a target for those who reject our ideals and seek to break us. We do not know enough about this latest threat to stage a robust, defensive effort. Therefore, I must, with the heaviest of hearts, advise that all home planets initiate global evacuation protocols. Fellow citizens, I urge you to remain calm and support one another as you make your way to the designated rendezvous points on your worlds. Where we're all going, there will be plenty enough room for everyone. Protector teams have been deployed to each of your planets to support your defensive forces, and assist them in holding off the coming attacks, which in turn will enable the evacuations to take place. I will not sugar-coat or play down the gravity of this situation, but believe me when I say that this is not the end. We must, for now, retreat and regroup to preserve our species. Hold on to each other and to your hope, help is on its way, and we will get through this. We are grateful for your cooperation, support and sacrifice. Time is short. For Peace."

Chapter Twelve

Evacuation

Zendara and Mardran had been sent to the southern side of the *Slaavene* homeworld to coordinate the evacuation. Thousands upon thousands of citizens were gathering. The ground beneath their feet began to rumble and quake. The jungle foliage shook violently all around them; rousing the vast colonies of native, nocturnal Winglings from their slumber, the commotion of which had sent them soaring in their hundreds… up through the dense jungle canopy, and out into the blinding light of the sun.

The drill-tipped nose of Pilot's Loway Pod breached the jungle floor, sending rocks and debris hurtling in all directions. Panic threatened to spread through the amassed citizens, as they backed away from the flying debris and heavy machinery of the pod. The pod hatch hissed open. The weight of it caused a heavy *thud* and *clunk* on contact with the alien ground.

"Friends, come dis pod for be safe," Pilot shouted to the masses, in a raw voice. Zendara approached the pod, shouting angrily in rage, "Pilot! You almost caused a stampede up here!"

"Pilot sorry friends, we need go now?" He flashed a gap-toothed grin at Zendara.

"You're not the Pilot I know," Zendara exclaimed, clearly confused.

"Many Pilot's, one name...all name Pilot. Come, we go." Pilot grinned again as Mardran approached the pod.

"How are all of these people supposed to fit into that pod?" she snapped.

"Pilot think you friend rude, Pilot here help. No more asking from you, must go...now" said Pilot, "We fit, you see, dis entrance. We go Core Loway, come." Pilot insisted.

"I apologise Pilot, we are just confused about how this works, and you did give us a scare with your entrance. Maybe some kind of warning next time?" said Zendara.

"Dis no ting worry, but this new friends they funny look, they like Lizgardia," said Pilot innocently.

"Well, they probably think you look like an overgrown Rangmouse," laughed Zendara.

"Dis fair ting you say," responded Pilot, with a jerking nod of his head.

Mardran had done her best to reassure the Slaavene Elders that they were here to help; the Elders in turn spread the word throughout the masses - explaining that they were going to be safe, and that they just needed to keep calm and follow instructions.

A show of faith was needed, so Dargrelle, (the head of the Elders), volunteered to enter the Loway Pod first. He was stunned by the sight that greeted his sceptical eyes. The pod was in fact nothing more than an entrance to a transport portal: the interior was awash with myriad, pulsating lights. This was a motion accelerator, and a direct route to the Loway via the planet's core. Dargrelle entered the pod, stepped towards the lights, and found himself being welcomed by Pilots, and a multitude of different species that were all standing on board the Core Loway… looking properly disorientated. Within seconds, more of his own people began to join him.

"Come, come citzen friends. Follow Pilots, make da room." The barrelesque Pilot shuffled towards the exit or entrance to the next compartment. The new arrivals followed on, slightly dazed, but relieved.

Chapter Thirteen

Defence

"It is good to see you again, Commander Raxnelle," Seventeen addressed his ally.

"Your sentiments are reciprocated Protector Seventeen. We look forward to fighting shoulder-to-shoulder with you once more," said Raxnelle, "...and please, just call me Raxnelle."

"As you wish...Raxnelle. We have received intel from Unity. The attack on *Shinara Prime*, the black smoke, it's all too familiar. This is the work of *The Hushed*; but they are different, evolved somehow... to inhabit living hosts." Seventeen was understandably melancholy.

"Yeah...and look how things turned out for them and their second-rate, mumbo-jumbo last time," quipped Zero-Nine, cockily.

"Do not mock *The Hushed*, Zero. They have been, and always will be, a real threat." Seventeen had assumed his usual serious tone.

"Pah! Hushed smushed. We beat them once already," Zero replied.

"Zero, old friend. You should be mindful of such frivolous comments. Please excuse his coarse rhetoric Raxnelle."

"Not at all, I like his confiden..."

An alarm screeched and cut Raxnelle's comment

short. He pressed his finger to his ear: "They are here…" Raxnelle shot an intense look towards Seventeen as he spoke, "Follow me, we will talk on the way. What else do we know of this new enemy?"

"Unity has advised us of some measures that may give us an advantage in the coming battle. Do I have your permission to brief your warriors on our plan of attack, and provide them with the necessary equipment?" asked Seventeen.

"Of course, time is of the essence, and we must be a unified force."

* * * * * * * * * *

A wave of black smoke slithered across the floor of the lush jungle, moving much like the serpentine Slaavene - slinking its way through the stunningly-treacherous jungle terrain. Powerful beams of red sunlight cut through the gaps in the leaves of the canopy, creating strong pillars of light so vivid, that they gave the illusion of being solid matter. The dark silhouettes of the hosts of *The Essence*, passed through the beams of sunlight in jolting, jerky motions, shattering the illusion of solidity with their intentionally-awkward and sluggish gaits. They replaced the false tranquil vision of the jungle with a grim new reality. *The Essence* meant to transform the *Slaavene* homeworld into another dull, black, suffocated sphere.

The Slaavene themselves, a proud warrior race, would not go down without a fight. The midnight-blue skinned Slaavene, had an advantage which most other species did not.

Their skin was a natural camouflage: an almost perfect match for the swirling black horror of the smoke and the horde. It allowed them to blend in and attack from within the enemy's numbers. The Slaavene were also a cold-blooded species, so they were not so readily detected as most other races of the New Unity. They had been briefed by Seventeen and had taken action accordingly, equipping themselves with bio-synthetic breathing apparatus to protect against the all-consuming black smoke, whilst maintaining their camouflage. *The Essence* approached, oblivious to the scores of Slaavene warriors slipping seamlessly from the cover of the trees and vegetation, and into the vast bulk of their army. The Slaavene stealthily infiltrated the collective, moving as one within their numbers.

Son Reynar oozed confidence as he strode deep within the press of the horde. He felt powerful, god-like, as he commanded these hideous beings once more. At the snap of his mechanical fingers, these lumbering creatures would transform into the swift, deadly, killing machines that he had used to end the traitor Taire on *Shinara Prime*. For the moment though, he was content with drinking in the power at his fingertips. They would stalk the jungle a while longer. Now that Taire was dispensed with, he wanted to savour the anticipation of the coming slaughter. The sensation was beyond thrilling. Reynar clenched his fist so tightly that his mechanical knuckles popped; sending a blush of vibrant-blue, synthetic-plasma, rushing to the surface of the skin of his mech-hand. He gained some odd pleasure from performing this action, and gazed down at his fist with a satisfied smile as the blue hues dissipated.

The Slaavene subtly implemented their
offensive. They manoeuvred amongst the horde,
slitting the throats of the lumbering *Essence*
hosts. Each slain body released plumes of the
black smoke, which darted maniacally about the
jungle, desperate to find a new host. Reynar
was so enthralled with bathing in his moment
of glory, that he had failed to notice the
stealthy thinning of his horde's·numbers. They
were depleted by half before he finally
clicked his finger and thumb to launch the
attack - even then he was blind to where the
enemy lay.

    "Raxnelle! Clear?!" Seventeen's voice
boomed.
    "Clear!" came the response, as Raxnelle
commanded his troops to retreat deeper into
the jungle. A torrent of blaster fire ignited
the gloom of the shady, jungle vegetation, and
ripped through the humid air - cutting down
countless hosts, and shredding them to
tatters. The black smoke from each kill rose
high into the jungle canopy, before darting
back and forth in search of a new host. The
blaster fire was relentless… up, down, left,
right, diagonal - all in a deliberate pattern.
Yet still *The Essence* came: wave upon wave of
possessed flesh, pushing forward relentlessly.
Reynar was unmoved by the resistance of the
Protector Droids. He stood stoic, and watched
on as his horde did their worst to obtain this
planet.
    "Target the droids," commanded Reynar, full
of malice and intent. *The Essence* pushed on:
wave after wave charged at Seventeen and Zero.
    "You are awfully quiet Zero. Should I

consider this an admission of poor judgement?"
said Seventeen.

"No, you may not. I'm just concerned about
how my two lady lovers will cope if I were to
die here."

"They are not your lovers, as you well
know, and I cannot believe that you continue
to be so puerile in the midst of an actual
fire-fight," snapped Seventeen.

"Wouldn't want to disappoint you boss,"
quipped Zero.

"For once, will you just concentrate?"
snarled Seventeen.

The Essence had learned the firing patterns of
the Protector Droids, and were now upon them
in vast numbers. Reynar knew that the droids
couldn't be infected by *The Essence*, so
crushing them under a sheer weight of numbers
was the only possible route to victory. He
planned to encase them in an impenetrable
shroud of black smoke and possessed flesh,
along with the rest of the planet. The
Protector Droids were overrun; despite their
best efforts and immense fire-power, they had
been bested by the vast numbers of the savage
horde.

"I apologise Seventeen. Despite what you
may think - I always considered you a
brother." Zero's words were muffled by the
immense weight pushing down on him, but the
meaning lost none of its resonance.

"Brother Zero," Seventeen replied, "We are
not done yet! NOW RAXNELLE!" he boomed.

Reynar stood marvelling at the work of his
horde. Rarvin would surely reward him
handsomely for his efforts here. Reynar's
moment of self-appreciation was cut savagely
short -a blast erupted from beneath the bodies

of *The Essence*, sending body parts soaring in all directions. Seventeen had successfully distracted Reynar, allowing Raxnelle and the Slaavene warriors to burst forth from the thick foliage and attack. In a slick, fluid motion, Raxnelle leapt from the cover of the jungle, drew his sabre, and sliced Reynar's head from his body. Reynar's still blinking eyes watched on, as his own body fell to the jungle floor in a heap. Without a second thought, Raxnelle immediately joined his troops in hacking through *The Essence*, to free Seventeen and Zero from the weight of their grasp.

Chapter Fourteen

An Ending For One?

Treelo huddled in the corner of an immense hanger, deep in the bowels of *Won'Kaat Station*. The only light in the pitch darkness was the metaphorical glimmer of hope in his heart. He wasn't sure how long he'd been here, but he felt completely vulnerable and utterly alone. His combat suit and Tek shielding had taken a battering - as he navigated the possessed horde that now populated the station, in a bid to reach safety. He had sent a warning across all friendly channels to avoid *Won'Kaat Station*: he could only hope that the transmitter on his suit wasn't damaged and that the message got out there.

Although he appeared to be safe for the moment, Treelo was in a desperate spot, and he didn't know how he was going to get out of it. The only thing saving him from becoming hyperthermic in this black, bitterly-cold place, was the warmth and insulation of his combat suit. He was fully aware that it could run out of charge at any second, leaving him with only the faintest glimmer of hope to cling to. No suit, no Tek shield. Treelo's eyes and mind were beginning to play tricks on him. He feared that *The Hushed* were present in this place. He had a deep, foreboding feeling

in the pit of his stomach, the same feeling
he'd had on the shuttle pod after Kan Vok Tah
had murdered Neela, and tried to kill him too.
In hazy memories of slipping in and out of
consciousness, he recalled the song he had
heard Tam singing on constant repeat that
fateful day.

Long after they had been rescued, Treelo had
finally plucked up the courage to ask Tam what
the song meant. He had told him it was a
Vee'laan children's song. It was used to ward
off *The Hushed* long ago, before they had grown
more powerful. Now, convinced that his Tek
shield had been compromised, in a fit of
desperation, he sang that song. In a thin,
trembling voice, he mouthed the words
shakily...

Don't hear their whispers.
Don't heed their call.
For no sway have they,
over that which is yours.

For we are strong.
Our bodies our own.
Only we command,
our flesh and our bone.

Make deep your breaths.
Close your eyes.
Seal your mind.
Let them not inside.

We see you not!
We hear you not!
We feel you not!
We fear you not!
No power do you hold over us!

"Oh, how we've missed that pretty little song, haven't we - my children of darkness?" Rarvin's laugh cut through the total blackness of the hangar. It was a chillingly cruel sound, filled with evil intent. A collective spine-tingling hiss emanated from the pitch dark that enveloped Treelo. "Things were much simpler for my children when the songs were your only defence. You have been a worthy prey, the last mortal standing, or should I say, cowering on this station, but none can evade my will." Treelo couldn't even muster a response, "Now my children, take him."

Hear our whispers,
heed our call.
For we hold sway,
over all that was yours.

The collective voices hissed and snarled the words with a deliciously evil joy.

For we are strong.
Your bodies we own.
We command,
your flesh and your bone.

Hold your breath.
Open wide your eyes.
Your mind is open,
We are inside.

Treelo recoiled, clamping his hands to his ears as he screamed out. A flash of brilliant white light backlit a horde of chillingly-contorted silhouettes.

You see us now!

were the words that accompanied the intimidating visuals,

You hear us now!

They were too close for comfort, as if being whispered in stereo, millimetres from his ears. Treelo's breath was taken away by the shock of an excruciating, searing pain that ripped deep into his stomach, like a blunt, jagged dagger of ice was tearing him open.
You feel us now!

Treelo screamed in terror and blind panic.

Aaah...yes, you fear us now!

The next words came in a sinister, smug whisper.

Total power we hold over you!

A thick, acrid smell filled his nostrils. He knew it was the black smoke of *The Essence*.
"No!" he screamed, "It can't end like this!" He exhaled hard, trying to expel *The Essence* from his nose and mouth. It was no use. As he slipped from consciousness, he heard the soothing tones of a familiar voice from his past.
"Trust me old friend, let go … this is the only way. Rest now...when we awake, there will be much work to do."

Chapter Fifteen

Prophetic Head

The Nomad was an older vessel, a fact that made it no less impressive. This was a classic, model six, hybrid-class ship, a model that had been decommissioned years ago. *The Nomad* was a fine specimen, in pristine condition. Greem had maintained her very well.

Tecta and Pilot were deep into their mission, and totally unaware of the events unfolding at home. Even if they did know, they would have had no choice but to push on. Vrin had made it abundantly clear that their mission was too important to abandon at any cost. They had travelled deep into unknown territory, caught glimpses of strange worlds, and thankfully, benign alien species and vessels.

   "Fly nice, dis Nomad," said Pilot, who was grinning from ear-to-ear, steeped in his natural environment.
    "Indeed. It was very generous of Greem to entrust her to us. Clearly this ship means a lot to him." Tecta was clearly impressed. Pilot had to apply all of his piloting savvy to follow the ever-changing path Vrin's tracker was plotting for them, making scores of micro-adjustments, thruster bursts, planetary sling-shots and sector jumps.

Piloting a vessel of this size was a world away from flying his Hornet, with its nimble controls and slick manoeuvrability, but he was loving every second of it.

"Friend Tecta, colour dis tracker change," said Pilot, with a touch of uncertainty.

"We must be close friend. Reduce speed, and I will run a scan of the area," Tecta replied.

"No need scan, look, see," said Pilot, gesturing to the view screen.

In the distance, there was an odd landmass that appeared to be floating freely through space. It didn't seem to belong to any system or group of planets. They were not sure it could even be classed as a planet. This looked like a dense collection of rocks, soil, and vegetation - encapsulated in an atmospheric sphere. It wasn't small by any means, just bizarre and alien in appearance.

"Head ting live there?" Pilot asked.

"This is where Vrin's tracker has brought us friend, so it must be the right place," Tecta replied.

"Ship go through bubble ting to make land?" Pilot's innocent curiosity led to him having a question for every imaginable scenario.

"Yes my friend, are you ready?" asked Tecta

"Yes friend Tecta, we make land."

"Any more questions?" asked Tecta, with a smile.

"Erm...Pilot no tink so."

"Good, take us in." Tecta was fascinated by Pilots as a race. At times they seemed utterly clueless, then in the next instant,

they were intuitive, selfless geniuses.
Pondering for too long on the mysteries of the
unique, diminutive race made his circuits
hurt.

The Nomad passed through the atmospheric
sphere untroubled, and Pilot expertly touched
them down in a vast field of long grass. When
they stepped out of the ship, Pilot was
overwhelmed by the sensation of inhaling such
clean air. It was cleansing. The aromas of
flora and fauna carried on the light warm
breeze. This place was tranquil and homely. It
felt safe. The peaceful ambience was
interrupted by Vrin's tracker bleeping sharply
once again in Tecta's hand; it displayed
steady, pulsating lights.
    "I guess we follow the lights," said
Tecta, "That way." He pointed to a sparsely-
wooded area ahead, and off to their left.
    "No worry friend, Pilot find dis Head."
Pilot stomped off as fast as his stubby legs
would allow, "Hello! Where you friend Head
person?" shouted Pilot.

As they drew closer to the trees, Pilot's
calls were answered.
    "I hear you small one. Ring the bell, and
I shall present myself." The voice that spoke
was muffled and earthy.
    "Oh, please," Tecta sighed.
    "Tradition is far too understated in these
current times," the voice of the Head stated.
Pilot gazed at Tecta, questioningly.
    "Very well, do as he asks friend," said
Tecta, nodding to a huge bell-like mollusc's
shell, that was partially obscured by
overgrown brush and colourful foliage.
    "Pilot, hit dis ting with what?" Pilot

looked at Tecta confused.

"With the beater of course," was Tecta's response. Pilot was clearly confused.

"The birds, catch one and you'll see," said Tecta. A number of curious-looking birds were hidden within the surrounding scrub. Pilot threw himself whole-heartedly into the challenge of chasing one of them down. Pilot chased and thrashed around in the thicket, like a thing possessed in his pursuit.

"Friend Tecta, this tings, they fast as fastest tings Pilot seen ever," said Pilot breathlessly.

"Patience friend, you will catch one. Be as they are, be still, and await the right moment to pounce." Pilot completely disregarded Tecta's advice, and continued his fruitless running and thrashing.

"Actually friend, some lessons aren't worth the wait." Tecta's arm shot into the scrub in a blur, and a bird was in his grasp instantly. It had become rigid, and now resembled a hammer or hatchet. It was a harmless defence mechanism of the species.

"So, this is why it's called a Hammerbill." Tecta's unintentional joke rose a slight chuckle from Pilot, as Tecta passed him the rigid creature. Pilot grasped the bird by its stiff legs.

"Hello, friend Bill," smirked Pilot, "Pilot sorry for dis." He swung the Hammerbill like a smashball bat, and it made solid contact with the shell…
Clang!!! The resonance of the unremarkable sound faded quickly.

"Thank you friend Bill," said Pilot, with his usual tooth- filled grin. He set the bird free, and it flew off perfectly, appearing to have no ill effects from being used as a beater.

The giant mollusc shell peeled slowly open to
reveal a giant humanoid head; adorned with a
mess of wild, knotted red hair, and a gnarled
overgrowth of facial hair that obscured almost
all of the Head's facial features. Deep brown,
almost black eyes, and a kind smile, shone
from within the mess of hairiness.

"You rang?" the Head bellowed, followed by
a hearty, rumbling laugh, "You seek an
audience?"

"We do, oh wise one. Vrin, of Lardoria,
has assured us that you can offer us advice in
our darkest hour," Tecta said, addressing the
Head respectfully.

"Vrin...ahhhh, it warms my nose to know
that she still breathes. I would say warms my
heart, but alas, these days I have not a
heart, just a head." The Prophetic Head's eyes
were briefly filled with sadness, as if
recalling a long-lost, much happier time. He
had the look of joy on reflection of these
memories, but it was coupled with the
realisation that they were just that.
Memories.

"What happen to Head body? Sorry, please,
sorry Pilot no mean ask," said Pilot.

"That is a question for another time that
I would gladly answer. But, right now, you
need to save your galaxy, do you not?" said
the Prophetic Head.

"Pilot sorry, friend Head. How we save
Unity, please?" said Pilot.

"Even before the Dawn Wars, the ancestors
of what you now call the 'New Unity', were
looking to the future. They prepared Spore
Pods of raw origin materials to send out into

space, in the hope that they would settle on distant planets and seed them with sentience. This was done in the hope of ensuring a future for the ever-growing population, and generations to come.

The Spore Pods drifted on the solar winds… being swept further and further away from their native galaxy."

"What happen friend, dis plan work?" Pilot was enthralled by the Head's storytelling.

"You must retrieve that which was sent forth to create these futures. Time waters down your origins, and spreads the source material thin. The source sent forth is the key to beginning again. If you cut off the branches of what you have, you're left with a trunk; but it's a solid trunk, as branches can regrow if spliced with the correct saplings. But, then again, what would I know? I've only been here, right here in this very spot…" The Prophetic Head momentarily nodded off - before giving a deep snore, which snapped him awake again.

"What was that?" he said, startled.

"That you friend, you snores," said Pilot bluntly.

"Me! Snoring!" said the Head, "That's preposterous! Anyway, where was I? Oh yes. I have been here, right here, in this very spot for so very long. Watching the rise and fall of so many 'civilisations', none of them particularly civilised I might add." He turned his attention to Tecta.

"You, metallic life-form, who is unsettlingly like the mortals you protect. You already know what comes next, and what you must do to save what you have built, in order to win the last conflict! Her return is at hand, and you must end her. It is the only way…"

"She is thought to be indestructible,"
said Tecta, bluntly. Pilot cocked his head
from side-to-side, completely bewildered by
the conversation.

"Every being has a weakness, and you have
already encountered that which can help defeat
her. You must make a friend of an old enemy,
to receive that which you need."

The Prophetic Head spoke frequently in such
riddles. Tecta opened his mouth to speak, but
the Head started talking again.

"One more thing; you have an ally on the
inside, within the darkness. This ally is
difficult to see, two people occupying one
space, caught somewhere between the dark and
the light. Remember this; you must trust this
ally. Look not only at the surface, but see
what lies beneath. I'm exhausted… this is the
most conversation I've had in centuries." The
Prophetic Head yawned long and deep, almost
inhaling Pilot, who was clinging tightly to
Tecta's leg, "Now go. Remember what I have
told you, and may the twelve systems bestow
good fortune upon you and your quest."

"Thank you for your wisdom friend," said
Tecta.

"Friend Pilot. I would very much like to
tell you my whole story, should you survive
and return to this place," said the Prophetic
Head.

"Thank you, Pilot think." Pilot was less
than full of confidence at the Head's parting
words.

"Him, Protectic ting, him nearly eat Pilot
and him speak funny, Pilot not understanding
tings him say."

"You're okay Friend Pilot, he meant you no harm, and riddles can be very hard to decipher. But, your wisdom runs much deeper than words. You will feel the meaning of his message. I'm sure of that. Come now, we must resume our journey."

"You know what him say? Where go us Friend Tecta?"

"We'll start beyond the Korrix System and Liquid Space… the Third System will be our first destination. That's where they took her," said Tecta cryptically.

"Who dis her and they you say?" Pilot was even more confused than usual.

"Injis and the Mora," said Tecta, solemnly. Pilot was stunned into silence.

"It'll be alright friend. It has to be. This is our only option," said Tecta, reassuringly.

"Dis plan bad friend Tecta, she bad, bad bad bad! She kill friend Fiddy-Six." Pilot drew a deep, contemplative breath and continued, "Dis what him Protetic ting say?"

"Yes friend. Injis is the enemy that we must make an ally. We need her weapon… *The Hunger*," said Tecta.

"See! Pilot say Head ting try kill Pilot, we see dis Injis gain, we dead!" Pilot stomped and gesticulated wildly - his anger was comical to witness, but it was very real to him. Luckily, Tecta had little-to-no sense of humour, so laughing inappropriately wasn't an issue.

"Friend Pilot, as I've said, he's not trying to hurt you. If you're scared or don't want to continue the mission, that's also fine. You can take the escape pod back to Unity." Tecta knew exactly what Pilot's next response would be.

"Pilot no scared no thing, Pilot need protect Tecta." Pilot's whole demeanour changed. He puffed out his chest proudly, before saying, "Why you wait friend Tecta? We need go." Pilot's actions and words raised a rare smile from Tecta; Pilots were a chaotic rollercoaster of energy and emotions in general, even more so when they were stressed.

"We had better go then friend...and I'm very happy you are coming with me," smiled Tecta.

"Pilot's duty dis is." Pilot's usual toothy grin had returned.

Chapter Sixteen

The Power Of Mora

"Lu has sent us a communication. The New Unity is under attack!" said Gliis, in stunned disbelief.

"What's happened? How bad is it?" Kee'Pah replied.

"It sounds dire, she has ordered the evacuation of all the sentient planets."

"We should head back to help," said Kee'Pah, her face etched with concern.

"No, Lu has ordered us to stay on course and consult with the Order. She hopes they might have some ideas, or even better, some solutions," said Gliis.

"We'll find out soon enough," sighed Kee'Pah.

"We've entered Moran Space. Prepare for our final approach and planetary entry," said Seventy-Five.

Mora was a spectacle to behold: the Order of the White Rock had grown strong and resilient on their reborn homeworld. They were an amphibious race - equally as comfortable on land as in the vast seas of this glorious planet. The people of this world knew the black smoke only too well, and they stood resolute in their belief that the insidious spirit of *The Hushed* would gain no ground here. Unlike the other planets of the New Unity, Mora and its inhabitants had developed the symbiotic existence that the other planets and their people still strived for. Mora, along with its people, were at least a generation ahead of the rest of the New Unity. They were united, and ready to defend themselves as one.

The elongated nose of their ship pierced through the cloud banks above *Mora*. The world before Gliis and Kee'Pah was unrecognisable, the entire surface was oddly changed. As they drew closer and gently touched down, it became apparent that the usually gently-rippling oceans had solidified to become a perfectly level, solid, marble-like surface. From space, the entire world was as a spherical blue glacier, but from their current position on the ground, the planet was littered with occasional dense, chalky, columns of Mora's now infamous White Rock.

It was completely barren - not a sign of life was to be found.
    "We need to get to the White Rock," said Kee'Pah, "I need to physically touch its surface, to communicate with the Order." The pair headed for the nearest column, where it loomed like an imposing monolith against the fast-moving, cloud-streaked sky. They had been walking for a good few minutes, but the rock didn't seem to be getting any closer.
    "Maybe we should have landed a little nearer," said Gliis.
    "We couldn't have known that the ocean wasn't liquid. We needed to land on solid ground. Anyway, stop your complaining, this is

beautiful and refreshing."

"And eerie, don't forget eerie," Gliis joked. A shrill digital chime sounded from Gliis' comms.

"Gliis, somethings not right… our sensors have gone haywire." It was the metallic monotone of Seventy-Five, one half of their Protector detail. As there were no apparent threats in the vicinity, Gliis had asked Seventy-Five and his fellow Protector counterpart to stay onboard the light transport vessel that had brought their group here, and continue to run scans.

From out of nowhere, a black haze appeared on the horizon, sullying the majesty of the pristine blue and white landscape. The grubby haze could be seen in all directions. It was an ambush… they needed to get to the White Rock - the haze was shifting at a rapid pace, and soon they would be surrounded.

"Twenty-Seven, Seventy-Five get your detail out of here now," commanded Kee'Pah. "That's an order."

"But, we can help!" Twenty-Seven shouted, breaking his regular monotone.

"Leave now, and do not open fire under any circumstances. We need to trust *Mora*." Kee'Pah screeched.

Gliis and Kee'Pah ran as fast as they dared, across the surface of the solid, aqua-blue sea, trying their hardest not to slip over. They needed to reach the white monolith. The ship's engines boomed as Seventy-Five engaged the thrusters. An even louder boom followed - in a flash of blinding light, the ship and its Protector crew were obliterated.

"No!" screamed Kee'Pah.

"There's no time, we cannot fail," said Gliis curtly, "We can't let their sacrifice be for nothing," he screamed, grabbing Kee'Pah's hand and running for their lives.
The kill shot was fired from orbit, and it had been unleashed by Azvoc. He chose to watch the killing of *Mora* from the comfort of his ship - no need to get his hands unnecessarily dirty.

Gliis and Kee'Pah finally reached the stark White Rock, and scrambled up its side. The second that they had reached their destination, Kee'Pah slapped her palms onto the rock's surface, and pleaded with the Order to help them. They were marooned, their ship and crew destroyed, and *The Essence* were closing in on all sides. The black haze grew more and more dense, closing in with every passing second. They could make out figures in the misty substance; and as it drew closer still, it transformed into a mass of black drool, gnashing teeth, and viciously-slashing, claw-like fingers. A sea of eyes, like dead-black mirrors, reflected the scene of the pair's seemingly hopeless plight back at them.
"Where are they, Kee?" said Gliis, his face taught with tension.
"They are here Gliis, awaiting the opportune moment," replied Kee'Pah, her voice calming and her constitution solid, following her earlier emotional outburst.
"Well tell them to hurry up!" was Gliis' stressed response.
"Gliis, look at me," Kee'Pah spoke calmly and reassuringly, "Remember the first time we met?"
"Of course. I'll never forget."
"You trusted me blindly with your life, to guide you to the depths of the Aqua-gel. I ask

you to trust me again now."
It was like a switch had been flicked in his
brain. Gliis' eyes lit up with renewed hope
and realisation.
    "We're bait, aren't we?" he whispered.
    "Took your time, my love," Kee'Pah
whispered back, followed by the sweetest of
smiles.

The crude rock they clung to began to rise,
carrying them up and up, beyond the reach of
the marauding hosts of *The Essence*. They could
feel something shift within the Aqua-gel sea.
All at once, the host bodies screamed out in
unison… agonising, blood-curdling screams
filled the air. The hosts were being absorbed
by the Aqua-gel; the Order of the White Rock
were dragging them down, into the depths of
the ocean. It was as if they had been dropped
into a vat of acid. The sounds of sharp
hissing and violent bubbling, replaced the
tortured screams and pained screeching of *The
Essence*, and in a matter of moments, all fell
silent…

A thin veil of black, grey mist hovered just
above the ocean's surface. The mist was
fading to white, dissolving with every passing
moment, and then it was gone - replaced by a
sea of countless humanoid life-forms. They
breached the ocean surface; coughing, gasping
and thrashing around to stay afloat. They were
all disoriented, terrified, and confused. But,
they were alive. The Order of the White Rock
had cleansed the hosts of *The Essence*, and
restored them to their natural state of being.
Now their strange amphibious saviours rose up
from the depths, to carry the cleansed beings
from the ocean to the safety of solid ground.

As soon as the cleansed were safely ashore, a strange light engulfed the skies of *Mora*, spreading from horizon to horizon.

"This cannot be!" Azvoc screamed ~~out~~ in frustration, "Fire all weapons, now!" his voice boomed. ~~but~~ The blasts from his weapons array were futile, fizzling like damp squibs upon contact with *Mora's* bio-shields. He had been outmanoeuvred. *Mora* had allowed him to deploy *The Essence*, and then was locked outside the atmosphere, sadly not before he'd taken out the Protector Droids.

This wasn't new to Mora; the planet had cleansed itself of this familiar enemy before, when Mora ceased to be the corrupted, coal-like planet *Exhilar*, and re-evolved to become the planet *Mora* once more. Gliis, Kee'Pah and the Order of the White Rock, were instrumental in that victory. Now they needed to find a way to repeat that feat on a system-wide scale.

"If the waters here can dissolve this *Essence*, surely the rest of the New Unity can use it to do the same?" Kee was sure that this was the answer they'd come here for.

"How do we get the waters to them?" said Gliis, "There are no ships on *Mora*. Even if there were, we don't know where that Raktarian battle cruiser is, and we wouldn't last a minute against a ship like that." The Order of the White Rock stood semi-submerged in the ocean shallows, collectively gesturing in the direction of the caves that lead to the Core Loway.

"Through the Core Loway, of course! We could use the water tanks to transport the antidote. Does the Order permit us to take some of the sacred waters from *Mora*?", said

Kee'Pah.

The Order bowed their heads, and raised their hands in unison. The sacred waters of the Moran Sea swirled, creating a great column. Gliis, Kee'Pah and *The Essence* survivors watched on in wonder, as the column of water majestically wove its way between them - in the direction of the caves.

"Thank you for this precious gift. You've given us a chance to help the home planets, and to return all these people that you've saved to their homes too."

Chapter Seventeen

Won'Kaat Station

Sin

The doors of the bar flew open, and the imposing figure of Rarvin loomed large in the doorway.

"The itch has been scratched Daa'Shond. Now we go to *Veela VI*, our victory is at hand," gloated Rarvin.

"Very good, my glorious leader, and I have wonderful news for you. Reynar has checked in, and the test mission was a devastating success. He also claims to have killed Taire of the New Unity." Daa'Shond was taking great pleasure revelling in Reynar's glory.

"It sounds like Reynar's mission was indeed a success. As for Taire, we'll see."

"He was adamant that he saw his demise with his own eyes."

"I have fallen fowl of Taire and his slippery siblings before. They are not to be underestimated. Has Azvoc reported in?"

"I'm afraid there has been no…" Daa'Shond's words were cut short by Rarvin.

"Azvoc, what is your status?" There was a long, static- filled pause.

"*The Essence* has failed to take hold, and the planet has become impenetrable. I have no choice but to throw myself upon my blade. I have failed you Rarvin."

"Do not judge yourself so harshly, and do not harm yourself. I have use for you yet. This galaxy has changed much since my last incarnation. They have clearly grown resilient, resourceful, and even more infuriating. I should have been prepared for this. Our approach must change. Make your way to the Planet *Unity*, and await further instruction."

"I appreciate your forgiveness Rarvin. I will not fail you again."

"I have complete confidence in you," sneered Daa'Shond, under his breath, "*Pfft, and I'm the one who can't be trusted with his own mission*," he continued.

"What was that?" Rarvin glared at Daa'Shond.

"Nothing, Rarvin sir - I was clearing my throat."

"Hmmm, that's what I thought."
The unlikely duo left the bar, and headed to the docking station, to board yet another of the Raktarian battle cruisers that Son Reynar had gifted to their cause. Rarvin's 'special *Essence* hosts' were safely stowed in the ship's cargo hold.

"This is a very fitting ship for someone of your status"

"I must admit, I am impressed. Son Reynar has proven himself a very effective and generous ally. I will name this ship *The Obliterator*." Rarvin eased himself into the luxurious captain's chair, and engaged the cruiser's thrusters. They purred smoothly out of *Won'Kaat Station's* hanger bay.

"A very fitting moniker." Grovelled Daa'Shond.

"Before we head out any further, allow me to ask you a simple question. Why are you still alive Daa'Shond?" Rarvin's voice was filled with menace.

"B,b,because I formed this coalition...maybe?" came Daa'Shond's stuttered response.

"Incorrect. Care to guess again?"

"You need my knowledge of Tecta?"

"Wrong again. It's quite simple really; when I'm done here with my mistress's bidding, I will need a domain of my own, to conquer and rule. You, my *friend*, will tell me all that I need to know to make your star system my own."

"Oh I will. I do so admire your ambition sir." Daa'Shond had been played and outmanoeuvred once again. He seethed at Rarvin's latest reveal. Every ounce of his being prickled and ached to rip Rarvin's head from his body, but he wasn't stupid enough to try and fight him head on. He needed to find an angle to exploit, and work his devious magic.

"Onward to *Veela VI*, my feeble-minded associate," Rarvin laughed cruelly, as the ship's engines boomed - sending them hurtling into hyperspace.

Chapter Eighteen

Veela VI

Evacuation

Nataalu had sent out a planet-wide alert, instructing all citizens of *Veela VI* to make their way to the Stadia Terranus. A Loway Pod and carriages had journeyed up from the core, and broken the surface of the planet. Lu and Tam were guiding the people of *Veela VI* aboard.

"Leader Nataalu, an unknown ship has entered Vee'Laan Space. Scans have identified it as a battlecruiser, same spec as the ship in Taire's report. What are your instructions leader?" Zero-Three made his inexperience glaringly apparent.

"Have you hailed them?"

"Of course, all protocols have been followed, but to no avail." Zero-Three's words were drowned out by a familiar sound - the distinctive whine and roar of Pilot's Hornets.

Overhead, the Pilot fleet powered into the sky, up through the atmosphere of *Veela VI*, then out beyond the planet's twin moons. Pilots knew they had to engage the enemy ship, or at least occupy it, until Nataalu got *The*

Unified airborne - with its significantly more heavyweight weaponry. If the cruiser was allowed to land on the surface of *Veela VI* and deliver *The Essence*, the consequences would be catastrophic.

"Pilot! What are you doing?!" Nataalu's voice raged from the comms, "You do not have enough firepower to take on a Raktarian battlecruiser!"

"Pilot be da Protector dis time," he croaked, "Pilot know dis, Pilot and friend Tecta away, say dis Pilot leader, dis Pilot have idea."

"If this is your idea, then it's a terrible one. It's suicide."

"Friend Leader Nataalu worry too much. Pilots make big ship busy, you Friend Leader Nataalu come, badda badda booom dis big one, baboom den big ship gone. Friend Pilot say him tink dat fishy tings comin' dis way. Him know tings. Pilot's fix dem tings good."

"Woah! Dis big ship, more big den city," squealed Co-Pilot.

"Pilot busy, go now Friend Leader Nataalu."

"But…," radio static crackled. Pilot had cut his comms mid- sentence.

"Zero-Three, get us up there now!" Nataalu barked.

"Leader Nataalu, we were not prepared for this. There is a process to follow. Our primary orders are to evacuate the planet and keep you safe," said Zero-Three, who was a less-experienced Protector Droid. At this moment in time, he felt completely out of his depth.

"I know, I know, I'm sorry. But please just do it as quickly as you can. Pilots need our help. Can we provide some cover fire from the ground at least?"

"I am afraid that the enemy ship's path is obscured by the twin moons. If we even minutely miscalculate our aim, or the moons orbit, then they could be destroyed."

"Aaargh!!!" Lu screamed out in frustration. She knew she'd brought elements of this situation upon herself. Sending her most experienced Protectors away may not have been the smartest move, but it was a necessary one. She had done what was best for the people, and she would need to find her own way out of this dire situation.

* * * * * * * * *

Pilots engaged Rarvin's ship like a swarm of angry-winged insects, twisting and turning with dizzying feats of aerobatics and darting attacks.

"Dis not so good, Hornets no make holes. Dis ting more hard den some hard ting." The Hornets were relentless in their efforts to inflict some damage, but all they achieved was taking more hits, spinning out of the fight, and then roaring straight back into the fray.

"Your aim is outstanding Rarvin. However, they seem to be quite indestructible, they just keep coming back."

"If I can't blast these things into atoms, I will find a way to shuck them from their metallic housings and devour them like slomp clam." Rarvin was furious, "What are they doing now?" he roared.
Pilots broke formation to split into two squadrons.

"Dis one cork da screw move, Zero-Nine

teach Pilots," croaked Pilot.

"Pilot try dis before?" asked Co-Pilot.

"No, dis Pilot's first time try." The two mini squadrons separated and positioned themselves at either end of Rarvin's cruiser. They engaged engines at full thrust, where one group encircled the body of the ship clockwise, whilst the other group anti-clockwise. The inertia increased speed with every revolution; it was vomit-inducing to behold, and the counter friction that the speeding loops generated, began to super heat the centre of the ship.

"What are those imbeciles doing?" snapped Rarvin.

"I'm afraid I haven't a clue."

"I wasn't asking you!! The question was rhetorical."

Two Hornets broke from the formation, one powered upwards, and the other downwards, away from the cruiser. They looped, turned tail, and roared back towards the centre of the ship, which was now glowing a warm orange from the counter-friction. They piled into the body of the vessel. Their nose-drills skidded across the surface, causing only minimal gouge marks and scoring to the cruiser's robust, armoured shell. Ultimately, the Hornets slid disappointingly off its surface.

"Pilot's go now, follow Pilot," screeched Co-Pilot. As he levelled his Hornet and followed Pilot's command, he vomited in his cockpit.

"Dis new move bad move. Zero-Nine trick Pilots, dis no funny," said Co-Pilot, then he threw up again.

"Him no dis, dis Pilot know dis, move fuse bad ones. Pilot's kill da time till Leader

Nataalu come."

    "Dis no funny, Pilot's more Gooder den dis."

Pilot's Hornet blazed away from the battlecruiser in a blur of black and golden yellow. His fellow Pilots held a tight formation behind him. The metallic sheen of their striking paint work pinged in the rays of the sun. The spectacle of the tiny ships, against the vast blackness of space, was a wonder to behold. Pilots felt the weight of their objective, but no matter how perilous their task, they would not waver in their determination to succeed. The survival of the small, burnt, orange planet far below them, was entirely dependent on their success. Pilots needed to keep the battlecruiser occupied, until the big guns arrived. The swarm of Hornets approached the twin moons of *Son'Tou* and *Mon'Tou*.

The monstrous bulk of Rarvin's battlecruiser was closing in on them fast. With every passing moment - *Mon'Tou*, (the larger of the two moons), grew startlingly closer, until its barren terrain filled Pilots' entire viewscreen.

    "Friend Pilots, dis nearly time. We ready try dis one more ting?" croaked Pilot.

    "We ready!"

    "What dis ting we do?!"

    "Pilots ready, do for friend Unity," were just three of the exuberant replies from his fellow Pilots. The silver, boulder-strewn surface of *Mon'Tou* was now in startlingly-sharp focus. Its majestic terrain sparkled, albeit briefly, before being swallowed up by the gigantic looming shadow of the battle cruiser - which now kept pace menacingly above the Pilot fleet.

* * * * * * * * *

"Do not underestimate these minuscule detritus, they have caused untold damage to my cause before," Daa'Shond hissed hatefully, without his trademark *M'wah* to be heard.

"But *you,* my feeble associate, are no warrior!" Rarvin's overly- confident, cocky demeanour had returned, along with his former blind arrogance. Both were back with full effect.

"Forgive me for asking, but what is your plan again?" Daa'Shond's voice wavered. He was already second-guessing the wisdom of questioning Rarvin's tactics.

"I'm almost impressed that you have the guile to insinuate my tactics are questionable." Rarvin's tone was too calm and measured for Daa'Shond's liking: he squirmed awkwardly in his seat.

"I, I meant no disrespect. I am very curious by nature. A flaw in my personality which I desperately need to work on." Daa'Shond was back-pedalling in panic. Rarvin sat, stony-faced, giving no response. His silence sent shivers down the length of Daa'Shond's spine. "I think maybe I should just shut up now."

"A wise decision," sneered Rarvin, who was now completely focussed on executing his plan.

He skilfully aligned the cruiser's multitude of belly canons to unleash a series of continuous energy beams. They merged to create a deadly perimeter around the swarm of Hornets - there was no way out, not even down, as the moon was too small to cope with the stress of the Hornet's drills. The friction would destroy it from the inside out. Pilots were trapped, encompassed by a stunningly-luminous wall of certain death.

"Genius, *m'wah*," said Daa'Shond, whose pinched nasal tone was filled with faux admiration, "Finish them!"

"I have something much more delicious in mind," said Rarvin, whose voice contained a foreboding glee. He activated the cargo bay door, releasing the thick black *Essence* and its hosts. It swirled and crept threateningly out of the hold. He switched to manual flight controls, and began an excruciatingly-slow descent; sandwiching Pilot's fleet between the unrelenting surface of *Mon'Tou*, and the dark twisted horror that descended from the cargo hold.

"Friend Pilots, we drill," croaked Co-Pilot.

"Where Pilots drill?" was the panicked response from another of the pilot fleet.

"Pilots drill up." Snapped Co-Pilot

"Pilots no drill smoke ting, dis plan bad plan."

"No," chuckled Co-Pilot, "Pilots drill up through da smoke ting and boom up dis ship."

"You friend Pilot head problems, dis fool crazy plan."

"Pilot shush!" Co-Pilot croaked firmly, "Three we go." The croaky Pilot had already manoeuvred his Hornet. It's nose drill pointed directly upwards.

"Stop! Pilots go three or go?" The question came too late, Pilot's count had already started.

"ONE!" On that first count, the whole Hornet fleet manoeuvred to match the croaky Pilot's position.

"TWO!" The whine of the little ship's nose drills rose, peaking in their familiar vicious squeal.

"THREE!" The boom of the engines came, the noise sounded way too big for the tiny ships that created it, yet the power contained in those minuscule units was immense.

"GO!!!!!" The Hornets rocketed upwards, launching a devastatingly-swift assault, and in a matter of seconds, they had not only just powered through *The Essence,* but also the thick metal ceiling of the cargo bay. The tiny ships continued their upward journeys, boring through a multitude of decks. Finally, the Hornets exploded out ~~of~~ from the top of the battlecruiser, and into the freedom of Open Space.

The battlecruiser below them now resembled a block of metallic cheese. Though it remained in one piece, it was peppered with breach holes, each one smooth and self-sealing. The bored metal was polished smooth by the intense heat generated by the nose drills. Oxygen hissed from the multiple breaches that the Hornets had created - the ship was de-pressurising fast.

"Report! Where did they go?" screamed Rarvin, as spittle sprayed from his furious grimace of a mouth.

"They appear to have drilled through the body of the ship, and they are now above us. I told you not to underestimate…" Daa'Shond's nonchalant diatribe was swiftly interrupted by Rarvin's hand - gripping his face and squeezing hard.

"Evacuate ship, life support critical in 10, 9, 8"… The cruiser's onboard systems delivered the warning in a flat, emotionless voice. Rarvin released his grip on Daa'Shond's face, as a second critical failure notice sounded, "Fuel lines ruptured, catastrophic ignition imminent. 7, 6,"…

"You will live through this you snivelling wretch, for one reason only… I may need currency to buy myself some time, and rare species such as yourself are of great value, even on a liberal, peace- yearning planet such as *Veela VI*. There is always a dark underbelly lurking… longing to find a way to break the monotony of their mundane hopefulness."

"…And don't forget, you can use me to take control of my star system! That's another good reason to keep me alive," stammered Daa'Shond pathetically, whose words were nauseating even to himself. The bridge of *the Obliterator* separated from the cruiser proper, with a sharp clank and hiss. Rarvin punched the boosters, they were away, and not a second too soon - the newly named ship had exploded in a spectacular light show. The energy fence that Rarvin had created failed, and *The Essence* dispersed harmlessly into the vacuum of space.

Chapter Nineteen

Seekers Return

"Pilot, you did it!" The communicae came not from Nataalu, but from Taire's ship *The Seeker*. They had finally arrived to help.

"Uh huh, Pilots do dis ting, but bad ones escape." Rarvin's escape craft blipped on their view screens, "Pilots now Unity Child, dis Pilot know what dat Pilots tink, dat Pilots know what dis Pilot tink. All Pilots know same tings, but different same time. No time talk. Friends need stop dat escape ting." The irony of his comment, and the length of time it took to deliver it, was lost on Pilot.

"Great job, friend Pilot, we're on it," said Sanvar. *The Seeker* had actually started giving chase shortly into Pilot's speech.

"Thank you for your bravery, but this is far from done," came Taire's familiar voice, ringing from the comms, "I need you to go on an important mission to the Broken Crown. Once you arrive there, conceal yourselves among the fragments, and keep watch over Unity for approaching threats."

"Pilots do dis, friend Taire." Co-Pilot's croaky voice was filled with pride.

"And Pilot!" said Taire sharply, "Once he returns, friend Pilot will be proud to hear the tales of what you did here today."

The Seeker thrust forward, firing all cannons

at full volley, but Rarvin's escape bridge was
nimble… twisting, turning, ducking and
spinning to avoid the incoming barrage of
fire.

"He's more slippery than a swamp Kreppen."
Grunted Sanvar

"How do we stop them?" said Nel

"Well, the usual salting them ain't gonna
work." Sanvar replied

"Track their projected landing
coordinates." said Taire taking control of the
situation "Pilots, report to Nataalu and Tam
on the surface, this isn't over yet."

"Taire, what are you doing here? You're
supposed to be helping on *Slaavene*?" said Lu,
joining the conversation.

"Heard my little sister was getting
trouble from bullies," Taire laughed,
"Besides, Seventeen and Zero-Nine have the
Slaavene situation under control. We'll take
care of things up here. How is the evacuation
going?"

"Slowly, but we'll get through this."

* * * * * * * * * *

Rarvin's escape bridge breached the Vee'Laan
atmosphere. *The Seeker* followed moment's later
- its forward cannons blasting volley after
volley of energy bolts. The peculiar looking
escape module still had a few more tricks up
its proverbial sleeve.

"What do we do now?", squealed Daa'Shond.

"Wait for it!" was Rarvin's curt response.
His fingers worked furiously at the console.
With a *hiss* and a *thunk*, the forward console
section of the bridge sealed itself, and
dropped clear of the main bulk of the escape
bridge - firing off covering chaff as it did

so.

"An escape pod within an escape pod?"
Daa'Shond couldn't disguise the excitement in
his voice.

"It seems the ingenuity of the Raktarian
race really does know no bounds - truly
exceptional engineering," said Rarvin, with
more than the slightest hint of admiration.

"Surely their scanners have picked us up as
two separate signatures by now?" Daa'Shond
said, sceptically.

"Always there with the snivelling and
whimpering aren't you? I've scrambled our
thruster signature, and sent the rest of the
bridge to lead them on a wild Grook hunt. We
will simply vanish for the time being.

* * * * * * * * *

The secondary escape pod drew ever closer to
the red, dusty surface of *Veela VI*.

"If you have a god, you should pray to them
that we land on sand, not stone." Sneered
Rarvin

"I did once have a god, but even if she
wasn't dead, I'd rather land on stone than ask
her for anything." Daa'Shond shuddered at the
mere thought of that vile creature.

"Brace!!!" Rarvin's command sounded steady
and unconcerned with their impending impact.
The escape console hit blessedly-soft sand,
bounced, rolled, then bounced again. The
gyroscopic interior of the pod kept the two
occupants on a steady level throughout. The
escape console slid to a halt, and hissed
open. Daa'Shond coughed dryly, at the
miniature sandstorm their vessel had caused to
swirl around them.

"Yes!" Rarvin exclaimed, "This is what I have yearned for. I feel so… ALIVE!!" he shouted unapologetically, "This is even closer than I could've hoped for," he said darkly.

"You mean - you planned for us to land here! Why?!"

"I wasn't planning on being here so soon, but since good fortune finds us here, I have a small matter of correctional wrath to attend to."

"I don't wish to be an annoyance, but you said we were to be single-minded in our mission, with no distractions."

"Do not question me. Our mission is fluid if it suits my needs. Descendants of *Feer'aal* dwell here in this region, and they have much to answer for," said Rarvin, as he strode ahead with purpose. Daa'Shond scrambled behind, shielding his unlidded eyes. The uncomfortable crunch of sand between his ample sets of teeth was grating, and extremely unpleasant.

"I'm not one to complain, but…" Daa'Shond complained.

"That's exactly what you are and exactly what you're doing, so silence that mouth, before I permanently seal it for you."

Rarvin had no time for Daa'Shond's typical Daa'Shond-ness. He had seen this part of *Veela VI* before, but only in the visions afforded to him by *The Essence* and *The Hushed* that came before them. The caves… *The Silence*… the treacherous R'aal. It was all, somehow, very familiar. How he despised those embarrassments - what a waste of Feruccian blood and bone. They would pay for their abandonment - of all that he and their ancestors had stood for and held dear. Rarvin felt the pull of Feruccian blood. However much the R'aal had tried to separate themselves from their brutal past, they could not separate themselves from their DNA. Rarvin sensed them, and sniffed them out like a tracker Voxen.

The R'aal returned to *Veela VI* after the Battle of Mora, and sealed themselves within *The Silence*, requesting that they be left alone. They would not be drawn into any more conflicts, and would dedicate themselves to their spiritual fulfilment. Not a soul had seen or heard anything from them since.

"Follow me, and try to keep up," Rarvin ordered Daa'Shond, as he began to scale the rocks. Not before too long, they came to a narrow opening in the rock face. Rarvin inhaled deeply, and let out a blissful sigh, "This way, I can almost taste them." Rarvin slipped inside the tight opening - Daa'Shond reluctantly followed…

* * * * * * * * *

Meanwhile, *The Seeker's* pursuit of Rarvin's abandoned escape vessel had ended in less than impressive fashion. The module came sputtering to a halt; and hovered benignly, unable to lead them on any further - its thrusters were spent.

"The pod is empty, and there's no bridge or flight console. I'm afraid we've been outmanoeuvred," said Sanvar, disappointedly.

"Not necessarily," said Nel, "The ship's log can tell us where they jettisoned the crew." Nel connected to the ship's computer and accessed the flight logs, "Here!" she said, pointing at the screen.

"That's *The Silence* of Vee'La," Taire sighed with worry.

"What's there?", asked Sanvar.

"The R'aal," Taire answered grimly, "We must warn them. Sanvar, set coordinates and initiate thrusters." The journey was a short one.

"There!" Sanvar exclaimed, as he pointed at the wreckage of the escape pod strewn across the rocky, sandy surface. *The Seeker* touched lightly down, belying the urgency of those within. The ship's hatch hissed slowly open, and Taire burst from the doorway.

"The seal is still intact," said Taire, quizzically, "Whoever was inside that pod has either found an alternative way in, or they are unaware that the R'aal dwell here."

"Let's hope it's the latter," said Nel. She was acutely aware of the worry that Taire was feeling.

The sands before them began to shift and swirl in circular patterns… a small, shelled, metallic being emerged from the sand.

Chapter Twenty

Aandrillians

Their existence had been hidden for centuries.
The Aandrillians were thought to be the
original, indigenous species of *Veela VI*. They
thrived in burrows far beneath the surface of
the planet, feeding on its bountiful supplies
of precious core metals, which they used to
bolster their impressive shells and natural
defences. If left alone, these creatures were
harmless, dwelling in, and snacking on, the
pay-dirt of the generations of miners that had
come and gone after them. If threatened, they
were more than capable of defending
themselves. Tam's reinvigoration of *Veela VI*
had stirred the Aandrillians from their
slumber - deep within the chasms and ancient
maze-like burrows of the Vee'Laan subterrain.
Now they sensed the purpose of their
unexpected rejuvenation.

"Fleshly youngling. Powers ancient of
Raktar enliven thou wielded weaponry do they
not? To these drawn are ourselves."

"You are very observant; fear not, we have
not come here for a fight."

"What say dis one, friend Taire? Him no
sense," said Runt coarsely.

"Manners Runt, it could say the same about
you."

"*Keesh keesh.*" The Aandrillian made a

unique laughing sound, "No battle do themselves seek, *keesh keesh*."

"Fortunate for themselves. Odd mix, know not ourselves skill or origin either," said a second Aandrillian, as it popped out of the sand.

"We are looking for a path to *The Silence*, and the people known as the R'aal. They need our help." explained Taire

"Unusual such congregation, odd of varied origin travels together. Which thoughts come to thou Schneb?"

"The ancient metals ourselves shall consult, to aid yay or nay, aforementioned congregation odd of varied origin that travels together."

"With thought of such agreement mine-self holds. Let us commune."

"Halt, and still you shall hold congregation odd of varied origin that travels together."

"Decision ours thou shalt await, patience upon yourselves ourselves must request."

"We understand your cautiousness. We will eagerly await your decision." Said Taire

Keesh keesh keesh, the strange pair snickered, as they curled themselves into their spherical metallic shells, and disappeared into the sand.

"What are they doing? We don't have time for this!" Nel protested.

Chapter Twenty-One

In The Silence On Veela VI

Rarvin and Daa'Shond reached the entrance of
The Silence.

"Wait here, and do not try to run."

"Can I not come with you? It's rather
unnerving in here."

"I will not show them any sign of weakness,
and that is exactly what you are, so do as I
say."

"As you wish. To be fair - I understand. I
wouldn't take me in there either." Daa'Shond
had truly lost any remaining semblance of
self-respect. Rarvin strode confidently into
the grand cavern.

"Show yourselves, cowards!" His voice broke
through the eerie hush that hung in the air.

"Who goes there?" asked Targole, (the
spokesperson of the R'aal), in a firm,
authoritative tone. He, and his fellow R'aal,
stepped into the natural illumination of the
cavern's gems.

"You have lost your way. You've forsaken
aggression, abandoned violence - you have lost
all that makes the Ferrucian race great. Where
is your urge to conquer and destroy? You sing
of peace, dance like fools, and indulge
yourselves in healing, love, and making
repulsive art on each other's skin. You call
yourselves R'aal? You have quite literally

taken the fear element out of your name and heritage - and discarded it. You disgust me!"

"I don't know what kind of maniac you are, or why you are so obsessed with Feruccian lore, despite not looking anything like a Feruccian. That uniform is a statement from an outdated, long, and best forgotten era: an era that brings us untold shame. Now leave this place! You are not welcome here…"

"Granted, I have a new, very different, and possibly even prettier face, but surely you can recognise the soul of the legendary warrior that dwells behind these eyes?"

"Your mind is clearly fractured. We abhor violence, however if pushed, then we will defend ourselves. So I repeat, leave this place now." Targole thumped the blunt end of his Electro-Pike into the ground - the friction of which travelled the length of the weapon, activating its point with a static crackle and fizz.

"Rarvin Cha!" Rarvin's voice boomed in thunderous echoing loops, filling *The Silence*. He unsheathed the Blade Of Ancients, and held it aloft.

"I will not leave here without a fight!" Rarvin lunged at Targole; who swept the strike away, ~~and~~ returning to his previous stance, Electro-Pike held proudly by his side.

The dance-like encounter continued with Targole, repeatedly deflecting - but never countering.

"You are a skilled warrior, but defence will only get you so far. Come on… strike, attack me! Maybe if I cleave you wide-open, I can find your true nature somewhere within your heart, and show it to your brethren, so that they may learn from your mistakes."

"You and your barbaric ways have no place here. I will not be goaded into retaliation." Rarvin's vicious attacks and Targole's subsequent deflections continued over and over, each ending the same way as the last - with Targole in his defiant stance, his Pike held fizzing and crackling at his side.

"Maybe you are like Rarvin. He too failed in his lust for violence. Now leave here."

"I am tired of this pantomime," said Rarvin, nonchalantly, "Let's move things along." He drew a vial of the poison from his inner robes, and slammed it into the ground, "Now, I will transform you into that which you fear the most... your true selves: merciless, blood-thirsty, Feruccian killers." Rarvin knelt, cupped his hands, and lifted them both to his mouth. He exhaled the insidious *Essence* into his cupped hands; then he drew his hands apart - and with fingers splayed and winding - he commanded *The Essence* to follow, as he twisted and turned his wrist. He led the dancing black smoke in winding loops, eventually coming to a halt in front of his face. He paused for a second, then roared, unleashing a gushing torrent of *The Essence* onto the bemused R'aal... who themselves murmured and smirked at the actions of what they thought to be an unhinged lunatic. Targole was the first to begin choking on the acrid smoke, followed by gurgling screams and wrenching among the gathered R'aal. The crowd's demeanour was transformed to one of wide-eyed panic and terror. Some of them took their own lives, in an attempt to avoid the same fate as their brethren, unaware that the act of doing so would make no difference. *The Essence* would take hold of them before their brain death. Rarvin roared with malevolent laughter, and hacked his way into the panicking R'aal, "Now, you will ALL… KILL… FOR RARVIN!!!!" Whilst *The Essence* did its work in transforming the doomed R'aal, Rarvin's attention was drawn to the pulsating walls of *The Silence*. He'd already admitted that his plan needed to change, now he had been afforded an opportunity here - one that he would make the most of.

Chapter Twenty Two

Aandrillians II

With a shiny, metallic *shing* sound, the Aandrillian pair sprung up from the sand - opening their shells.

"Comprised of materials similar," Schneb's comment was directed toward Nel, "Thou self, he plus I. Relatives distant conclude ourselves to be, agreement to aid ancient metals afford to congregation odd of varied origin that travels together."

"Are you saying that you two and Nel are related?" asked Taire.

"Spoken such truth we have to odd mix," said Boopf.

"Odd mix?" questioned Nel.

"Find offence, will yourselves should ourselves address congregation odd of varied origin that travels together, as odd mix? Events will hasten if agreeable the name you allow," said Schneb.

"Odd mix is agreeable," replied Taire, "Will you show us to the R'aal please, Schneb?"

"Name of Boopf, mine-self. Schneb, name of the other," said Boopf.

"Apologies," said Taire calmly.

"Friend Taire, no apologise. Dis tings make problems, talk much, no useful!" Runt was losing his patience.

"Runt, that's enough. Schneb and Boopf

have offered to help us."

"Dis good, but Runt tink dat more quicker be more good." Taire was so happy that Clint had been agreeable to staying with Sanvar back on *The Seeker*. His input, along with Runt's, could've been catastrophic in this muddled conversation.

The Aandrillians had started moving ahead of the group.

"Odd mix, ourselves, yourselves follow fast." Said Schneb and Boopf in unison.

"That's rich!" laughed Nel.

"*Keesh, keesh, keesh*" the Aandrillians laughed, "Cousin, joke yourself makes, pleases ourselves does this. Aandrillian's the best jokes ourselves make, the metals cause these they must."

"Cousin?" Nel felt a welling up of emotion inside her that she had never known, save for her feelings for Taire. But this was different, this was a connection at a core level. She had found a people that shared part of her physical DNA.

"Ourselves of the metals are created, many layers we have. You too have, ourselves and yourself family," said Schneb.

"Thank you, cousin Schneb," said Nel. Saying those words out loud made her feel giddy. She was experiencing the alien sense of belonging.

As the group of unlikely companions traversed the maze of subterranean tunnels the Andrillian Schneb told the tale of his species beginnings.

"Ourselves awakened by planets sentient for assistance of yourselves. For much time ourselves slumbered. Of Veela as yourselves name, ourselves are part. Aandrillians here from commencement of Veela, as yourselves name." said Schneb

"Take much time, find deez Raals?" Runt grew ever more impatient. He still didn't trust Nel, and now he was stuck underground with her distant relatives.

"Are there more like me?" Nel asked, ignoring Runt's grumbling.

"An army ourselves - long ago built from the metals, to defend all Unity once began the Dawn Wars, much like odd mix their appearance. To *Raktar*, for enlivening themselves were destined, ourselves observed the actions and treachery of *Raktar*, to themselves, ourselves could not entrust this powerful, ancient metals army. A prototype themselves did then build, ourselves believe Nel cousin ours to be said prototype. Enlivened with the power of good Nel has become. Themselves on *Raktar* failed in their corruption, as did Qa'Xeera, the Dark Mother herself, fail to corrupt Nel." Schneb spoke passionately.

"How do you know all of this?" Asked Taire

"Ancient metals, things aplenty themselves know concerning all the metals." Schneb replied

"Is this Qa'Xeera of the ancient metals?" Taire asked

"Created of our ancient metals she was not!!" He was furious at the very suggestion, "Of the darkest of all forbidden metals herself was created!."

"Apologies friend, I meant no offence." Said Taire

"At *The Silence* ourselves and yourselves have arrived, though I fear bad news ourselves must reveal to odd mix." Boopf sighed

"What bad news?" asked Nel.

"Odd mix yourselves must see," said Schneb heavily. The two Aandrillians led the odd mix along a narrow snaking passageway the group rounded a corner to emerge into an expansive cavern, it was eerily silent - the floor slick with blood, and black slimy residue. They were too late… the cavern in *The Silence* was empty, (except for the butchered remains of a few of their number). The R'aal were gone… Taire deduced grimly from the carnage that this was *The Essence*; his friends and allies were already turned, and they were loose on *Veela VI*.

The cavern felt wrong somehow, like it was dying. Natural gems were fading, and veins of darkness infiltrated the walls. *The Silence* had stopped pulsing and undulating. Something was very wrong. He would need to call on Gliis and Kee'Pah, as this was their area of expertise. Firstly, they needed to locate and take out *The Essence*.

"Apologies, ourselves make to yourselves, the metals advise yourselves could prevent this not. Odd mix leader yourselves Sister, still yourselves can help, as ourselves can yourselves help." Schneb's words were the cue for a flurry of action.

A multitude of Aandrillians emerged from the shadows, and began to spin like band saw-blades, eating a passage through the dense rock of *The Silence*. Even Taire's mythical rings could not cut through the solid surface at such a pace. The small, metallic creatures were so swift, that the bright rays of the sun were soon flooding the newly-carved passages with glorious, life-giving light.

Chapter Twenty Three

Awake

"Treelo, don't freak out, we're aboard your ship. Ambassador One: that's a snappy name...Ambassador Treelo. Wow, things have changed."

"Neela, is that you?" said Treelo, who felt groggy, like he was in a hazy fog, "I can hear you, but I can't see you. I can't see anything!"

"Just breathe, you're okay…"

"Wait…you're dead! How can we be speaking, am I dead too?" Treelo's voice was filled with panic.

"So many questions, but no, you're not dead," Neela laughed sweetly, "What do you remember?"

"I was hiding in the cargo bay, my combat suit's energy source was depleted, so I sang the old songs to ward off the evil that surrounded me. I didn't know what else to do. That black smoke and those undead things were getting closer every second...pain, fear and then… you, your voice."

"There only one course of action that could save you. So I did the only thing I could, or you would be dead."

"Do I want to know what that 'only thing' was?"

"I joined our consciousnesses: we are as one…but only for now."

"You were one of those things and you've possessed my body? You should've let those things kill me."

"No, that's not how this works, calm down and let me explain. If I hadn't joined with you, one of the savage ones would have taken control of your body, and you'd be one of those mindless 'undead things' as you called them. As I said, it was the only way to save you."

"So, I'm not one of those zombie things?"

"No, you're not one of those zombie things. You are sharing your mind and body with *me* though."

"Where's your own body?"

"You already know the answer to that question. You witnessed my death, remember? Coincidentally, you also witnessed my rebirth."

"The one that rose and stood staring at me, whilst the others tried to tear me to shreds, that was you?"

"Well deduced my friend, you're still sharp."

"So, what happened to that body?"

"When I woke in that body, I was in complete control, unlike the savage souls who are completely lost and insane. They act on impulse: the impulse to kill. I could've occupied that body permanently, and escaped to somewhere far away from here. However, when our eyes met, I saw what you did to Kan Vok Tah, and I felt what you felt. You paid a high price to avenge me. I couldn't let you die after seeing that. I abandoned that other body to save you."

"Neela, thank you. I am truly grateful, but I'm very confused. How is this even possible?"

"*The Essence*: they are the latest incarnation of *The Hushed*, and the memories and consciousness of those that *The Hushed* controlled before they died. Now, if you're ready, I will retreat to your mind, and you will regain total control of your physical self. We will be able to communicate with thoughts, as we are now. Just think of me as a computer program running in the background. I will be able to see, hear, and experience everything that you experience."

"Seems a little intrusive – luckily, I have nothing to hide."

"I'm glad you have a sense of humour about this, it's gonna make this experience a whole lot easier. Maybe now is a good time to tell you that I thought I'd left it too late - that I'd lost your consciousness completely."

"What do you mean by that exactly?"

"Hey, don't give it another thought. You're here now, aren't you? Your combat suit is recharging. I have a feeling that we'll both be needing it. What's our next move?"

"Wait! How long was I gone?"

"Hard to say… four, maybe five rotations. But as I said, you're here now. So, what do we do? I'm a little out of touch."

"We go to the Children of the New Unity, if we're not too late." *Five rotations*, he whispered, in shock.

"The Children of the New what now? And by the way, whispering doesn't work here."

Just keeps getting better, Treelo whispered again.

"Uh, I can still hear you," laughed Neela.

"I'll fill you in on the way, so much has happened since…" Treelo paused awkwardly.

"Since I died? It's okay, you can say it." Neela's light outlook and openness were refreshing, "While we're talking about the past. What became of Tam, did he survive?"

"That's where we'll start then, but I will warn you, you are going to both love and hate the answer to that question."

Chapter Twenty Four

Showdown In The Stadia Terranus

Nataalu, Tam and their Protector detail were so engaged with the evacuation, none of them had realised that a savage threat, the likes of which they'd never seen before, was approaching. *Veela's* bio-shields rose to take shape around them, and seal them inside the Stadia Terranus. At that moment, they became acutely aware that something was amiss.

Rarvin commanded *The Essence* from a distance, like a general of old, viewing the battle from up high. The horde ripped through the homesteads, maiming and infecting any living beings they encountered, dooming them to join their ranks. *The Essence* was indiscriminate in its savagery; the blood-curdling screams of men, women and children echoed throughout the narrow streets, before giving way to screeching, overlapping voices - as the slain became one with the rampaging horde.

"Do you not want to be a part of the savagery Rarvin, you know, hands on?"

"I'm not ready to reveal my true identity to them just yet. I will make them suffer to the point of submission, and then I will reveal to them who the creator of their downfall really is, and will literally bloody my hands when I rip out their hearts."

"Is this part of the grand plan? I feel

you may have gone a tad off-piste, if you don't mind my saying so. It sounds very revenge-focused, and it might be blinding you to the bigger picture. I have heard whispers that you serve a higher being, and that is why you have been gifted your second coming." Daa'Shond had forgotten his place, he had taken no care in his choice of words.

"Do you never just shut up?! I am nobody's puppet. *The Hushed* may have tricked me last time. This incarnation however, I will use their gift against them, and their would-be-Empress, to take my rightful place in my galaxy. I wouldn't expect a creature such as you to understand."

"You underestimate my ambition, Rarvin. I have a deadly army of my own, patiently awaiting my orders."

"Would that be the hive of insect beings loitering on the edge of this system?"

"I, I, I'm not sure what you mean," stuttered Daa'Shond. Clearly, he'd been outmanoeuvred again.

"Allow me to show you," said Rarvin, who activated his holo-display, and replayed the moment that he and Azvoc infected Daa'Shond's Sectoid army with *The Essence*, merely hours before making their way to meet him on *Won'Kaat Station*. "One shot and game over. A very poor excuse for a back-up plan," Rarvin laughed at Daa'Shond, cruelly.

"How did you know?"

"When you have allies as slippery as yours, some level of betrayal is a given."

"Where are they now, my Sectoids?" Daa'Shond asked hesitantly.

"The hideously beautiful things that they became were in the cargo hold of my ship. I'm sure you recall how that ended, it was but hours ago. Do you not wish to know who betrayed you?"

"It is irrelevant," said Daa'Shond, who was broken, and Rarvin revelled in that fact. Those Sectoids were his last link to home, and the sense of loss was devastating, even for a scoundrel such as he.

Rarvin watched through his Binox, as the black smoke and possessed bodies of the R'aal and the Vee'Laans surged towards the Stadia Terranus, spewing their blanket of darkness over the desert world's surface.

"I see you." Rarvin's tone was a seethed whisper.

"Who?" Daa'Shond asked.

"The girl Nataalu: disobedient child - turned leader of a galaxy. Oh my, she does not comprehend the horror that is about to befall her fragile kingdom."

* * * * * * * * * *

The planetary shielding that encompassed the Stadia was failing… it glitched and phased, unable to maintain any prolonged stability. Nataalu had gathered as many citizens as she could inside. She felt the weight of responsibility for each and every one of them. Now, as the bio-shields began to fail inexplicably, she, Tam, and the Protector Droids formed a perimeter around the innocents that occupied the Stadia Terranus. They waited impatiently to board the Loway Pod and get to safety.

Burn bright - Nataalu kept dwelling on the choice of words Tecta had used in the training grounds. Could he have been alluding to her literal Vee'Laan inner-light?

"Tam." Nataalu sat cross-legged on the dusty ground, a vision of calm amongst the chaos, "Come to me." Tam responded immediately, he sat down opposite her and mirrored Lu's position. Instinctively, he knew what she meant for them to do. "We need to try," she said, with a knowing look. They both placed their open palms onto each others, and gently pressed their foreheads together. *Burn bright*, whispered Nataalu. *Burn bright*, Tam repeated. The two of them lit up, as they had on their first encounter so many years before, channelling the energy of their home planet. Their combined inner-light generated a brilliant, pulsating, white sphere. It grew larger and larger, caressing the two of them. Then it began to spread outwards… encompassing the citizens gathered inside the Stadia.

* * * * * * * * * *

"That concludes our business here. The planet's bio-shields will be down imminently, and they cannot keep that barrier up forever. When their energy depletes, *The Essence* will devour them, and take control of this planet. Onward to *Unity*."

"I mean no disrespect, but should we not make sure that they are definitely finished, before we move on?" Daa'Shond asked tentatively. Rarvin had heard enough; he was convinced that his plan would succeed, and he had no further use for the negative presence that was Daa'Shond. He drew the Blade Of Ancients and held it aloft. The blade made a threatening *vwoom* as it sliced through the air. The weapon's arc ended with a humiliating slap - as the flat of the blade made contact with the squealing Daa'Shond's backside. The force of the blow sent him flailing and rolling down the vast dunes. Rarvin watched on with a malicious grin, as Daa'Shond tumbled and slid toward the Vee'Laan homesteads below.

Rarvin needed to get to Unity. In order to do that he needed a ship, since his own was utterly destroyed. He scanned his immediate surroundings, and as good fortune would have it, Taire's ship *The Seeker* was close by on the opposite side of the mountain. He only detected one life sign on board. Rarvin took his leave, and receded into the boulder-strewn, mountainous terrain … he needed that ship.

* * * * * * * * * *

Taire blinked into the light. The sight that awaited him was one of utter chaos. Droves of black smoke and *Essence* hosts surged through the Vee'Laan homesteads, and on towards the newly-gifted Stadia Terranus. They appeared as a tsunami of hot black tar. He unleashed the rings into the slew of blackness, and followed them into the chaos - wrist blaster blazing from one hand, and the defence ring gripped firmly in the other. Nel followed suit, launching her component parts into the fray - each of them a deadly weapon in its own right. This unique ability allowed her to be in multiple places at once, which in turn improved their chances of even making a dent in the expansive horde.

On exiting *The Silence*, Runt stood dead still.

His hackles were up, but not for the same reason as his friends. He had sensed something unsavoury and familiar: he was completely overwhelmed with an uncontrollable sense of rage and anger. *Daa'Shond*, Runt whispered under his breath, as he rocketed out of the newly-formed cave entrance. He was headed in the opposite direction to Taire, Nel and the Aandrillians. He could smell the odious scent of his former captor, and in that moment, he realised that his opportunity for some payback had arrived. However, solo missions were not the Pilot species' forte, and his planned thirst for sweet revenge could soon turn sour. In a moment of unabashed rage, he grasped a sharp rock in the three digits of each of his small hands, and headed towards Daa'Shond's scent… his nemesis came into view in the distance.

Daa'Shond got to his feet, rubbing furiously at his lidless eyes in an attempt to eject the agonising grains of sand. After a few long moments his vision had cleared, but he couldn't quite believe what he saw. Runt was charging, fearlessly towards him.
    "Well, well, well, look at you. How adorable, *Mwah!*". Yes, Daa'Shond was a coward, but he was also aware of the physical and psychological advantage that he had over Runt. After all, he had spent years mentally abusing the diminutive life-form.
Thomp!! A rock slammed into Daa'Shond's head - searing pain shot behind his eyes, and he crumpled to the floor. In a flash, Runt was upon him - smashing at his face with another sharp rock.
    "*Mwah, mwah, mwah* ah ha," Daa'Shond laughed, as Runt's short arms ran out of

energy, "Oh dear, you seem to have failed in your vengeance. But, you have succeeded in giving me a chance. *Mwah!*." Daa'Shond threw Runt under his arm, and ran in the direction Rarvin had headed. Runt squealed and screeched, gnashing his blunt teeth at Daa'Shond, but he was agonisingly just out of reach, and totally helpless.

Chapter Twenty Five

The Seeker

"Who are you?"

"I am your new captain, now lay in a course to the planet *Unity*."

"You can't just walk onboard and steal my ship."

"Either you lay in the course, or I will kill you and do it myself."

Clint watched on from beneath an adjacent alcove, fighting every impulse to get involved and help his friend. He knew the smart move was to wait and let the intruder believe that Sanvar was alone.

* * * * * * * * * *

Nel stopped in her tracks, noting the absence of Runt. She stood statuesque amongst the violence of the running battle that raged around her, zooming her ocular implants, scanning the homesteads and dunes to find a sign of him. Her aural processors picked up a distant sound.

"Wait!" Daa'Shond's feint nasal tones sounded in the distance - "Wait," he repeated, "I have leverage."

There he was, a distant speck on the horizon.

Nel matched the visual to the audio. She recalled her component parts and immediately broke into a sprint, slicing through *The Essence* as she pursued Runt and his captor. Nel was fast, but not rapid enough to reach her targets before they boarded *The Seeker*.

"You picked the wrong people to mess with," she raged, and fired her fist at the ship. The fingers of her detached hand curled around the ship's closing boarding hatch, and once they'd locked on, she recalled the rest of her body's component parts. Nel was completely reassembled within a matter of moments. She planted her feet above the hatch, and levered it open just wide enough to slip inside. She hit the floor, already in her combat stance with weapons hot.

"Stand down she-bot, or the small one dies." Rarvin gestured to Runt - who was being held aloft by Daa'Shond's flipper-like hand, which was gripping him tightly around the neck. Nel cut a deflated figure, as the whistling/whirring noise of her cannons began to slow.

"You," Rarvin addressed Sanvar, "Fit our party crasher here with an inverter charge."

"But..." Sanvar didn't finish his sentence as Nel cut in.

"It's okay Sanvar, do as he says." Sanvar approached Nel cautiously, clutching the charge unit as gently as possible.

"Sorry Nel, hold still. If you try anything, this thing could go off, and fold you in on yourself like a crushed tin can."

Clint did the only useful thing that he could at this moment.

* * * * * * * * *

Taire was still in the throes of battle,
repeatedly launching Ki'resh to do its work,
and engaging in hand-to-hand with the trusty
defence ring Ve'dow. The Aandrillians were
tireless in their abrasive, spinning assaults
on *The Essence*. They appeared as multiple,
bladed discus - ripping through *The Essence*
hosts. But they were no one-trick species.
Clusters of them would sporadically spring
open and launch flights of metallic spines
from their bodies, like a company of archers.
Their combined efforts were slowly thinning
the horde, but there was no way that they
could defeat them all before they reached the
Stadia.

Chapter Twenty Six

Showdown In The Stadia Terranus II

Nataalu gave Tam a knowing look. He followed the unspoken order to brace himself, and she detonated the light sphere that they had created. The result was a spectacular sub-sonic anti-boom; all sound was sucked from the air, as the exploding light from the sphere unleashed a shockwave that ripped through *The Essence*. An eerily silent cleansing of the darkness and destruction that surrounded them swiftly followed. The bodies of *The Essence* hosts had been so horribly mutilated by Rarvin and the ravages of the battle, that there was no way a single one of them could have survived the separation from the black smoke.

The realisation that Nel and Runt were nowhere to be seen - hit Taire like a sledgehammer to the guts. He immediately thought the worst, scouring the dusty, tar-strewn battlefield and the fallen bodies that littered it, hoping not to see any sign of them. If he couldn't see them, then there was a chance that they were still okay. His comm bleeped; the sight of Clint's name as the message sender and the words… *Nel and Runt on Seeker*. He slumped to his knees in relief.

"They're alive," he exclaimed. His elation was to be short-lived, as he continued to read the communicae, "Danger, need help. Enemy taking us to Unity." Taire got to his feet and Terranus, where Tam was sat on the ground with Lu slumped across his legs.

"Tam, is she okay?" said Taire, breathing hard.

"She's just exhausted, and needs some time to recover," Tam calmly replied.

"How did the pair of you do that?"

"I have no clue," smiled Tam.

"Whoever did this has taken *The Seeker* and is holding our friends hostage. Nel got a message to me, saying that they are headed to Unity. I need to take *The Unified* and get there now."

"We'll come with you."

"Lu is in no shape to travel. Stay here, keep her safe, and make sure she recovers fully before trying to do anything."

"You can't do this alone."

"I'm not alone. I have Nel, Clint, Runt and Sanvar on the inside."

"Lu's not going to like this."

"Tell her - I'm just doing what's best for them. She'll understand."

Chapter Twenty Seven

Broken Crown

The Pilot fleet approached the Broken Crown. "Co-Pilot remember dis place," croaked Co-Pilot, "Pilot no touch, Pilot no touch," he laughed, remembering the now legendary tale of Pilot's first encounter with The Link in *The Silence*. He missed Pilot, and hoped for his safe return soon. The agile Hornets navigated the Broken Crown with ease, spacing themselves out and touching down on various rocks along its arc.

Co-Pilot landed inside the largest of the rocks, which was the former base and hideout of the Protector Droids. He peered out through the cockpit of his tiny ship, and was deeply concerned by what he saw.
   "Tings wrong here, no lights in dis caves," Co-Pilot croaked into his comms, "Pilots, any lights in you friends caves?" The answer to his question was not the one he wanted to hear. The Link was dead across all of the natural structures that made up the Broken Crown. The walls of the caves had once been alive with pulsating, vivid lights. But they had been replaced by dead, matt-black surfaces, solid and cold.

"Pilot, this is Taire. *The Seeker* will be in

your vicinity imminently. She has been hijacked by the enemy and they are holding my crew hostage. Do not, I repeat, do not engage them. Stay where you are friends. I will give further instructions when I get to you."

"Friend Taire, dis place broken, dark. Da Link no touch, ting gone." He wasn't entirely correct in his comments - The Link did light up sporadically, briefly bursting the caves into life.

"Try to stay calm friend, I'm sure that there's a reasonable explanation. For now, I need you to hold your position, and please don't try to fix anything."

"Pilot hear friend, Pilot no touch. Pilots wait." As Co-Pilot spoke, the familiar whine and squeal of a Hornet nose drill sounded.

"No Pilot! Dis no good plan," came the panicked voice of another Pilot through the comms. Mercifully, Taire had already cut his comm link.

"Pilot fix dis Link, light in dis walls." The grinding sound of metal on solid rock was teeth-clenchingly grating. The nose drill of the Hornet began screaming under the stress of the friction.

"Friends, what happen?" Co-Pilot was frantic, and he wasn't getting any answers or sense from his brethren. A mechanical jamming, jolting sound banged and clanked across the comms, followed by a blood-curdling scream, "NO!" screeched Co-Pilot, but it was too late. An impetuous Pilot had panicked, and took the decision to try to drill through the wall when The Link illuminated - and tried to time it right. But he got it all wrong; the drill of his Hornet jammed in the virtually impenetrable surface, and it was stuck fast. The pressure from the drill jamming was so immense, that it broke the body of his Hornet free from its stabilising clamps, and as the drill could no longer turn, the body of his ship started to spin violently. The friction and velocity of the spinning ripped the body of the ship away from the nose drill, sending the Impetuous Pilot hurtling into space. The rest of the fleet had no choice but to listen as the disastrous events unfolded.

"Pilot okay?" said Co-Pilot, his croaky voice breaking the stunned silence, "Pilot okay?" he repeated.

"Pilot okay… Pilot tink." Pilot's voice had a slurred and groggy quality from the disorientation of the high velocity spinning, and the brutal impacts with the interior of his ship.

"Pilot, get back in dis caves. Dis Pilot deal wid you Pilot later." For all the fury in his tone, Pilot was just relieved that the idiot Pilot was alive. In the commotion, the whole fleet had failed to notice *The Seeker* passing stealthily by, and landing on the planet *Unity* below.

The Unified, piloted by Taire, came into view.

"Friend Taire hear Pilot?" croaked Co-Pilot.

"I hear you Pilot, any sign of *The Seeker*?"

"Pilot no see no ships. All tings good here," Pilot cringed, at his bending of the truth.

"That's odd, I'm reading the signatures of *The Seeker* and a Raktarian cruiser on the surface. At least you didn't have the temptation of engaging them I suppose. Is everything okay? Any sign of The Link steadying?"

"All tings good, but Link off on still,"

said Co-Pilot, clearing his throat nervously.

"Okay, hold position. I have ordered the Protector detail on Unity not to engage. We can't take any risks whilst they have our friends held hostage."

"Good luck friend Taire. Pilot here for friend Taire if need Pilot help, okay?" Taire couldn't help but smile at Co-Pilot's good-hearted words, even though he was about to enter a viper's nest of unknown potential horrors.

Chapter Twenty Eight

Moran Loway

Gliis and Kee'Pah followed the column of water as it wove its way toward the Core Loway. It was majestic to behold, the undulating waters had a pearlescent quality - in hues of metallic blue and white. The column stopped at the entrance to the Loway, swirling and waiting. Gliis and Kee'Pah took the survivors aboard. The order had been communicated to Kee that the Moran waters would follow the Loway carriages, and they would follow Kee's instructions.

Barely minutes into the journey, the Loway carriage began to shake violently, throwing the passengers in all directions.

"Gliis, we have a problem. The Loway is pushing back against us," said Kee'Pah, sounding concerned and puzzled in equal measure.

"What? How? That's impossible!", quizzed Taire.

"Well, let me put it another way then. The Loway is trying to eject us."

"*The Nothing* wouldn't allow this!"

"Some things are beyond the control of *The Nothing*… it is not all powerful." The rumbling and friction intensified: the carriage was losing this fight. They were stunned by a violent jolt.

"Everyone strap in and brace yourselves!" Taire shouted, just in the nick of time - as the Loway carriage was forced into full reverse. They were hurtling back towards *Mora* at breakneck speed.

Chapter Twenty Nine

Veela VI

Catastrophe

Lu opened her eyes to see Tam looming over her, his face a picture of concern. The effort of the energy blast had wiped her out. It also appeared to have drained *Vee'La* itself. They had won this battle, but she could feel that something else had been lost. Lu looked around at the forlorn faces of the Vee'Laans. The planet felt wrong. Something about the terrain and the air itself had changed. What had felt so alive, vibrant, and hopeful merely hours before, now felt dead. It reminded her of the early lives she and her siblings had lived inside the Tek shield with Tecta, so desolate and barren. But Tecta wasn't here, and how she yearned for his comfort and guidance right now. He had to return and he had to have a solution.

"Where is Taire?" she asked Tam, weakly.

"He has gone after Nel and Runt. Whoever attacked us took them and *The Seeker* during the battle. Nel got a signal out before they jammed her communications, she said they are headed to…"

"Unity," said Lu, grimly, "We need to help them." She tried to sit up as she spoke, but she was still too weak from her earlier exertions, "We need to go to them now, we have to help!"

There was no time to dwell on what she could've done, or how she could've prevented any of this. Nataalu knew that she needed to get to *Unity*, the namesake of their new collective, and the home of the Unity Spire. It would be the ultimate target for whoever was controlling the dark forces that had attacked the Stadia Terranus.

"Taire said you need to rest, and that he is just doing what is best for you and our friends."

"Of course he did," Lu smiled, "But I am still leader, and I say we go now. I'll rest on the way; and I suggest you do the same, as this is far from over."

"Okay, as you wish, my leader." Tam gave her a wry smirk - he knew there was no point in arguing.

"One more thing," said Lu, "How come you're not feeling like this?" She gestured towards her utterly drained self.

"You and *Veela* did all the hard work. I think that I was just a signal booster of sorts."

The ground started to shake… the shaking grew more violent by the second. It felt as if the planet was going to crumble beneath their feet. With a deafening crack and the sequel of metallic friction, Loway Pods and carriages erupted from the depths of *Veela VI*. They had been ejected from the Core Loway; forced up through the planet's inner layers of rock and sediment, until they breached the surface – only to lay helpless on the dusty surface of the Stadia Terranus. All at once, every manner of species burst from the carriages in utter chaos and confusion, fearing for their lives. Others clamoured and screamed, in panicked attempts to rescue their loved ones, who were trapped inside.

"We have to help them!" exclaimed Nataalu. Tam jumped to his feet.

"Stay here, you're too weak to…" Tam's words tailed off, as Lu sprung to her feet and instinctively ran toward the chaos. The Protectors were already in the thick of it; some guiding the fleeing survivors to safety, while others charged into the Loway carriages and pods, to assist in freeing any trapped or injured citizens."

Chapter Thirty

Planet Unity

Taire guided *The Unified* smoothly to the surface of *Unity*, touching down a short distance from *The Seeker*. He left *The Unified*, and stealthily made his way to his beloved ship… walking cautiously up the open ramp… He headed directly towards the bridge… but there was no one there.

Blunkt brapt came the sound of those familiar tones, and it filled Taire with such warmth and happiness.

"Clint!" he exclaimed, "Are you okay?"

Brapt brunt blap.

"The others were taken, taken where?"

Blankt brrpt splankt

"Great Hall, but you hid. Great work little friend. Now I'm gonna need your help. Firstly, let's see what we are dealing with." Taire lifted a pair of Binox to his eyes, and scanned the area around the ship. As he scoured the horizon, the Great Hall came into view. His eyes were met with the first display of power from the enemy. He couldn't quite believe his eyes. Two precise lines of Feruccian warriors, in full military uniform, stood on guard at the entrance to the Great Hall. His stomach dropped - as he caught sight of Sanvar being ushered into the grand, palatial building. His hands were crudely-bound, and he looked badly beaten.

"Thirty-Two, do you copy?"
"This is Thirty-Two."
"Feruccian warriors are here on the planet, guarding the entrance to the Great Hall."
"This is a most unexpected and unwelcome development. We have other problems here; Loway Pods and carriages are erupting from beneath the surface, people are panicking, running, others are trapped inside. What are your orders Taire?"
"Continue with your rescue efforts. I can take care of this."
"You don't mean to confront them alone?"
"I'm not alone, I have a good friend with me."
"Good luck Taire, for peace."
"For peace, my friend."
Brunkt blap brapt, chirped Clint.
"I missed you too little guy. You've been very brave, but this is not the time to catch up. We need to get to Nel and the others. You can tell me about the people who took *The Seeker* on the way. I need all the information you can give me." Taire stowed Clint, who was still chirruping excitedly, in his pack - and exited the ship.

Chapter Thirty One

The Broken Crown II

The Impetuous Pilot had joined one of his brethren in their Hornet. It was snug, but it was a much better option than being exposed in a broken ship. The Pilot fleet had listened with dread to Taire's conversation over comms with Thirty-Two.

"Co-Pilot! Friend Taire need help," snapped the Impetuous Pilot, "Dis plan good, Pilots need try more times. When wall flash, Pilot drill."

"You Pilot head problems, Pilot near kill self. Dis no help no one," Co-Pilot said furiously, "Dis pilot order you Pilot no more try dis crazy tings."

"Dis Pilot help fix dis Link." The Impetuous Pilot was determined. He watched for patterns in the fluctuations of the wall, "Now dis Pilot go, for Friend Taire."

"NO!!! Pilots forbid dis!!", croaked Co-Pilot. It was too late…

The Impetuous Pilot had timed his window, and this was his moment. He engaged his nose drill, initiated thrusters, and blasted straight at the wall. His timing was dead on: the nose of his Hornet made contact at the precise moment. The black wall gave way to the wash of brilliant colour that was The Link.

The Impetuous Pilot, and his squashed Pilot brother, were riding the Core Loway. This was no ordinary journey on the Loway, it was violent and tumultuous. The tiny ship had a narrow, twisting band of Loway route to follow, and everything else was jet black. The sensation of the blackness was closing in around them… trying to swallow up the remaining Loway thread. It was claustrophobic and terrifying. The Impetuous young Pilot couldn't let it get to him, he was determined to succeed. An exit point lay ahead, but there was no way of knowing which planet the exit to *The Silence* would lead to. He couldn't navigate this treacherous route for much longer. Before he could veer towards the exit, the ship was ejected unceremoniously from the Loway. The Hornet burst from *The Silence*, and its nose drill immediately ground its way into the roof of a cave. Moments later, blinding sunlight flooded the cockpit.

"Pilots okay!! Pilots alive!!" the Impetuous Pilot screeched and pounded on the flight console. The fellow Pilot was speechless - a deep gulp was the only sound he could muster.

"Pilots incoming," came the familiar croaky voice of Co-Pilot, crackling from the comms. Hornets powered out of the hole that was now in the roof of the cave that housed *The Silence*.

"See, Dis Pilot say dis work!!" The Impetuous Pilot didn't even try to disguise the pride in his voice.

"Pilots lose Pilots on dis fool mission," Co-Pilot croaked.

"How happen dis?" asked Impetuous Pilot.

"Some Pilots follow through da Link, dis

Pilot follow dem Pilots. Now not know where Pilots gone, Pilots go out anudder way."

"Pilots strong, be okay. Help friend Taire and Protectors, den find udder Pilot friends."

* * * * * * * * * *

Taire prepared to approach the Feruccian guards.
I am here to speak with the leader of The Essence. He practiced his opening statement while composing himself. His thoughts were interrupted by a familiar sound, which was the roar and whine of Pilot's Hornet fleet. He watched in amazement as two of the miniature ships broke formation, and burrowed into the ground. It quaked and rumbled violently - as the Hornets powered along beneath the surface. The Feruccian guards fired volleys of blaster bolts into the ground, in an effort to stop the Hornet's subterranean assault. The two ships broke the surface, just a few metres in front of the guards. The guards continued to fire at them as they darted in and out of the tree line, weaving, looping, and feigning attack runs.

Clint made a joyful, shrill, whistling sound.
"Yes, they're distracting the guards. Hold on tight - we're going in..." Taire sprinted to the front of the grandiose building, and slipped past the guards to gain entry. As he stepped inside, it felt unsettling to be back in such familiar surroundings, yet in very unfamiliar circumstances.

Chapter Thirty Two

Confrontation

He traversed the overly-long corridor that led
to the Great Hall, and stepped boldly inside.
His footfalls echoed around the scantily-
furnished room. At the far end of the hall
stood Rarvin, facing the rear wall, with his
hands linked behind his back. He was flanked
by Daa'Shond/ Runt on his left, and Azvoc/Nel
on his right. Daa'Shond and Azvoc eyed him
cautiously, as they held on tightly to their
respective hostages. Sanvar stood alone, not
far from Runt, facing the wall, still bound
and trembling. Clearly Rarvin deemed him
harmless and not a threat.

   "Try using those rings of yours - and my
associates here will kill your little pet, and
the droid will be detonated. They will both be
dead before you can get anywhere near them,"
Rarvin spoke smugly, as Taire weighed up his
options.
   "By the way, I love what you've done with
the place." Rarvin turned around and faced
Taire, "And look how you've grown," he
continued, mocking Taire condescendingly, "Oh!
You don't recognise me? I'm hurt." Rarvin
laughed as he strode boldly from side-to-side,
holding Taire's gaze.

"I don't care who you are, we will stop you right here, right now," Taire spoke confidently.

"Ha ha haaaaa… we? You seem to be very much alone," laughed Rarvin, "You are Taire, correct? The non-fighter. As I recall, the last time we met - you were more concerned with mopping up our mother Etala's blood than fighting me." Rarvin smiled wide and cruelly., "You left that task to your siblings." Rarvin turned his back on Taire, as a show of fearlessness. Taire's entire being was rocked by the realisation of who the person standing before him really was.

"Rarvin! How?", demanded Taire.

"Your Protector isn't the only one that can stage a surprise comeback. Speaking of Tecta, where is he? He's not going to pop up and blow my head off again, is he?" Rarvin feigned a paranoid look-around with mock fear, "Oh yes that's right, he ran away, and not for the first time from what I hear." Rarvin was caught off-guard by Taire laughing.

"Do you not remember? It was I who delivered that fatal head shot, not Tecta." His composure was regained.

"Childish fantasy," said Rarvin, waving Taire's comment away dismissively, "But the time for such fantasies is over. This time you will fight me, or you will die... Actually, who am I kidding? You'll die either way."

Old habits had totally regained their grip on Rarvin: he believed once more that he could be the all-conquering warrior.

"Our mother wished your presence had never soiled her womb - you are pure evil," spat Taire.

"Why thank you for the compliment, however

flattery will not save you." Rarvin flashed a threatening, malevolent grin.

"You talk too much!" said Taire, dismissively. He tapped the rings together, producing a resonant chime. They were lifeless. Taire didn't let his face show the surprise and disappointment that this caused. The rings were devoid of their powerful green glow and Taire's connection with them had been severed. He knew that they were still deadly weapons, with a keen-bladed edge. Taire didn't have the luxury of time to figure out why the rings had lost power. He would need to improvise, and employ all those years of training with Tecta to win this fight - the old-fashioned way.

"Oh, aren't you all full of pith and vinegar, now take your best swipe at me…brother," Rarvin laughed out loud. Taire knew better than to be goaded into a naive attack. Instead, he circled Rarvin, spinning the rings between his fingers, waiting for him to lose patience and attack.

"Is this boredom-inducing display supposed to impress me?" Rarvin sighed - and was about to deliver another puerile insult. However, Taire took the opportunity to strike; he launched Ki'resh far beyond Rarvin and held Ve'dow in a defensive stance. Rarvin lurched forward, and simultaneously drew the Blade Of Ancients. He slashed from low-to-high, then from high-to-low. Taire deflected, and sparks flew. He stepped back, pre-empting Rarvin's lunging attack, but he switched it up, and launched into a spinning attack. Taire barely had time to readjust his feet, as he back-pedalled and deflected the vicious incoming strikes. Rarvin moved seamlessly out of his third pivot and into a full-blown lunge and thrust. Taire was ready; he shifted his weight onto his back leg, and trapped the blade of Rarvin's weapon within Ve'dow. He twisted and turned the defence ring, locking Rarvin's blade inside Ve'dow - then side-stepped - he struck either side of the defence ring, at opposite ends, with the heel of each hand. The Blade Of Ancients over-flexed, and snapped in two. Ki'resh hurtled through the air towards the back of Rarvin's head. He heard the whistle of the attack ring just in time - turning and ducking as it was about to strike him.

"Ha! You missed," hissed Rarvin.

"You were never the target," said Taire, straight-faced. Ki'resh found its true target, clanging against the dense, bony skull of Daa'Shond... he reeled backwards, dazed and disoriented. The searing pain caused him to release Runt from his grasp.

"So this tiny, furry thing is going to help you defeat me?" smirked Rarvin.

Nel twitched as she watched on. Azvoc stood close behind her, detonator remote in his hand. Nel was acutely aware that if she made a wrong move, she would be detonated and implode. The thought of buckling and crumpling in on herself - filled her with terror. But, would sacrificing herself give Taire a distraction... an edge?

Blunkt braaa brapt," bleeped Clint. The stealth mode he had previously deemed useless, had actually proved very useful indeed. He had disengaged the detonator attached to NEL, completely unnoticed. She immediately struck a sharp blow to Azvoc's face with her elbow — the dank thud of metal against bone was a sickening sound. He was out cold before his body hit the floor. Nel launched herself into a slide across the floor, to join the fray.

"No, but she will!" Taire looked down, and Rarvin's eyes followed. Nel smiled up at him from the floor, gave a cheeky wink, and punched him directly in the groin. Rarvin squealed and bent in two.

"Oh, so you didn't cut your new pair off," she said, smirking as she rose to her feet, "Maybe not so self-confident this incarnation?" She laughed, regaining her familiar combat stance.

"I will end you ALL!" Rarvin roared, in unbridled rage, unleashing bellows of the black smoke.

"Your parlour trick won't work on us, we are protected against it," Taire said with confidence - he knew that the Tek would nullify *The Essence*.

Rarvin ran screaming at Taire, and Nel stepped forward to intercept.

"No!" said Taire firmly, with authority, "He came back from the dead for this, he deserves a fair fight."

"No he doesn't. He's an abomination!" With a static fizz and crack, a blaster bolt slammed into Rarvin's back. He thudded to the floor, revealing Nataalu standing behind him - her wrist blaster still raised and glowing from the bolt she'd unleashed.

"You're too late," wheezed Rarvin, "You've already lost." His lips were stained with coughed up blood. He dragged himself to his feet, "You may think you have saved your beloved planets, but your precious Core Loway is dead. I saw to that, when I unburdened your treacherous friends the R'aal from their pointless, tedious lives in *The Silence*. The Dark Mother's time is near: she will destroy all of you…" Rarvin stood unsteadily, wielding the broken Blade Of Ancients. Taire and Nel stared at him, unsure if he was telling the truth. Rarvin lunged at Taire in a desperate final attempt to kill him. The scream of Nel's cannons intervened, with a violent volley of bolts that ripped Rarvin in two from groin to head.

"And this time - stay dead," seethed Nataalu. Rarvin's innards resembled the diseased lungs of a life-long Reed smoker. Tar-like globules slowly oozed from the catastrophic wounds that Nel had inflicted on him.

"Thank you, both of you," said Taire, who smiled at NEL and Lu, but something was clearly wrong. Lu looked anguished… it was etched all over her face, "What's wrong Lu? We defeated him… didn't we?"

"He was telling the truth." Nataalu's voice cracked and broke as she spoke. Taire's smile faded as she continued, "The surfaces of *Veela*, *Slaavene*, and here on *Unity* - have all been breached by quakes, caused by Loway Pods and carriages being ejected from the Core Loway. The evacuees are fleeing the carriages. The Protector Droids and Pilots are assisting them as we speak. So yes, I'm afraid it's true: the Core Loway is dead."

"Excuse me," came Daa'Shond's weak, groggy tone, which broke the silence, "May I make an observation? Rarvin has cleared the way for the Dark Mother to return, but he had been hatching his own plans to overthrow her. Now you have removed him and his treacherous plans from her path, you may have won her favour, and that is not to be sneered at!"

"You truly are a treacherous, deceitful, snivelling slime. No wonder Runt wanted to hurt you so badly. Maybe we should let him loose on you for a while, let him have a little payback." said Nel as she glared at Daa'Shond's battered and bruised face, which now sported a gruesome, open gash across his forehead.

"Actually, looking at the state of you, he may have already got some."

"You will answer for your actions against us, and if the Dark Mother does return…we will certainly not throw ourselves upon her mercy. We will do what we always do… Fight!" said Taire defiantly, "Sanvar, please take him away."

"My pleasure, Taire," said Sanvar – as he led Daa'Shond away. Runt gave a low, threatening growl as they passed by.

Chapter Thirty Three

The Third System

Tecta and Pilot had journeyed far and wide to locate the Prophetic Head, but they both now found themselves in more familiar territory. *The Nomad* had entered the Korrix System. They passed through the region of space where *Antipathy* had formerly been located. Rocky debris, and remnants from the destruction of *Antipathy*, harmlessly struck *The Nomad's* hull. This prompted Tecta to share with, and recall to Pilot, the full story of the events that had taken place during his imprisonment on the battle rock. He recounted his capture, the arena battles, the hideous God, and the vile Daa'Shond.

Pilot loved a good story, and Tecta's tale did not disappoint. It was a tumultuous stream of emotions - from the hopelessness of Tecta being alone so far from home, to the elation of victory in the arena, Tanque's diabolical demolition of God… right up to the ingenious rescue, (of which Pilot had been an integral part), and then the eventual destruction of that forsaken rock. The story had taken quite some time to tell, and they were now at the threshold of Liquid Space. The rift between spaces bubbled and swirled, filling their viewscreen as it swallowed up *The Nomad*.

"Friend Tecta, dis no look safe," said
Pilot.

"Pilot, there is nothing to fear. This is
where Daa'Shond captured me. I don't remember
much about being here, as I was in hibernation
mode. However, I do know that Liquid Space
itself did me no harm. The only perils in here
are the black hole at its centre, (which I
might add we are a very safe distance from),
or any unfriendly life-forms that may be
passing through," said Tecta reassuringly,
"And we are taking the shortest route through.
We will be in the Third System imminently." He
seemed to have reassured Pilot somewhat, and
then engaged maximum thrust. The gently-
swirling colours of Liquid Space exploded into
long streaks of vivid colour, as the ship
accelerated and sliced through the dense
fluid.

"Wow, dis beaut, beauta...erm dis pretty,"
said Pilot, staring in wonder at the
viewscreen.

The hypnotic spell of Liquid Space broke - as
the ship breached its boundary to enter the
Third System. Tecta powered down the
thrusters, to allow the scanners some time to
map and survey the system. When the star
charts were complete, Tecta and Pilot
identified which of the native worlds might be
able to sustain life.

"There," said Tecta. With a thick,
metallic digit, he pointed to a tiny speck on
the chart. The mapping process had detected a
distant planetoid that was emitting minimal,
natural energy readings, and appeared totally
devoid of any technological signatures. "That
has to be the homeworld Tanque chose for his

people. Plot a course friend, let's take a
closer look."

Chapter Thirty Four

The Planet Po'Tu

In The Phase Realm

"Qa'Xeera, your dream is about to become a reality."

"Please make this good. I will not tolerate any further failures or excuses from you."

"The anomaly Rarvin has exceeded our expectations. Not only has he betrayed us and put his own plan to rule *Unity* into action, he has also paralysed the sentient planets from the inside."

"And where is he now?"

"He is dead Qa'Xeera."

"Excellent. The Phasing is upon us… He has cleared a path, and the time for my return has finally come."

The End

The Unity Chronicles will conclude
with:

Qa'Xeera

The Last War

Book Five of The Unity Chronicles

Acknowledgements

This book is dedicated to all the strong, amazing women in my life who have been the inspiration for many of the strong female characters in The Unity Chronicles. My amazing Wife Lisa Mann, my awesome Daughter Annabelle Mann, my brilliant Mum Gillian Chuter and my fantastic Mummy in Law Chris Mann.
Love you all millions xxxxx

Special thanks as always to the studious Mr Michael Smith for your editing services and advice. Special thanks also go to the extremely well read Mr Geraint Llewellyn for your proof reading services and chats around ideas for the series.

Lastly, but by no means least. A huge thank you to ALL of you who have cared and been interested enough in these stories to pick it up again. I know it has been a bit of a wait for book four. Your patience and continued support are very much appreciated.

Printed in Great Britain
by Amazon

86246683R00099